some kind of magic

some kind of magic

Adrian Fogelin

PEACHTREE
ATLANTA

Published by
PEACHTREE PUBLISHERS
1700 Chattahoochee Avenue
Atlanta, Georgia 30318-2112
www.peachtree-online.com

Cover design by Nicola Carmack
Book design by Melanie McMahon Ives

Printed in February 2015 in the United States of America by RR Donnelley & Sons in Harrisonburg, Virginia
10 9 8 7 6 5 4 3 2 1
First Edition

Library of Congress Cataloging-in-Publication Data

Fogelin, Adrian.
  Some kind of magic / by Adrian Fogelin.
    pages cm. — (Neighborhood novels)
  Summary: In their last summer before the big shift to high school, Cass, Jemmie, Ben, and Justin find a mysterious hat which leads them to an abandoned builidng with a tragic past that might just nudge open the door to the future for all of them.
  ISBN 978-1-56145-820-2
[1. Neighborhoods—Fiction. 2. Mystery and detective stories.] I. Title.
PZ7.F72635Sm 2015
[Fic]—dc23
                                        2014041872

For the kids and volunteers of the Front Porch Library

Special thanks to my friend Mackenzie Moore-Adams.
You're an inspiration!

And thanks, as always, to the Wednesday Night Writers—
Jan Godown Annino, Gina Edwards, Noanne Gwynn,
Leslee Homer, Leigh Muller, and Linda Sturgeon—those
patient listeners and honest critics who are more
helpful than any magic hat.

SUNDAY
(seven minus seven)

Cass

It was the first day of summer vacation—well, second, really. But Saturday didn't count since I'd had to help Mama clean house. Jemmie, my best friend, hoped summer would go by quick. She couldn't wait to get to high school, where we could run track for real.

My kind-of-boyfriend, Ben, wished he could skip summer *and* high school and hit the road. All he needed was a license. And a car. And no little brother to watch.

His best friend and shadow, Justin, would do whatever Ben did.

Me? I wanted to run track for real, sure. But I knew everything was about to change. High school would be different. I liked things the way they'd always been in the neighborhood.

Just the way they were today.

We were all together, shooting hoops in the street in front of Mr. Barnett's, taking shots at a rusty hoop left over from his grown-up kids.

"Say, Cass!" yelled Ben's little brother, Cody. "You know what day it is?" He swung around, hugging the ball. "Don't tell her, Ben!"

I pushed my damp bangs off my forehead with the back of my arm. "The start of summer vacation?"

"No!" Cody crowed. "It's seven minus seven!"

Jemmie brushed a hand across Cody's buzz cut. "Equals zero?"

"N-O! It's my seventh birthday minus seven days!" He looked down at the ball in his hands, bounced it once, then hugged it again.

"Go on!" Ben clapped twice. "Take your shot while you're still six."

"Oh, right. Sure." Cody swung the ball between his legs a couple of times and shouted, "Hey, bop-a-loo-bop!" which he says is lucky, and let it fly.

"Oh man," Ben groaned as the ball sailed right over the backboard and landed on the roof of Mr. Barnett's carport.

Cody twisted a fistful of his surfer-dude T-shirt. "Oops?"

Ben trudged over and rapped on Mr. Barnett's door. The knock set off the old man's two yappy little dogs, Killer and Lillian, but Ben had to ask permission to climb onto the hood of his pickup to get our ball—everyone said Mr. B has a gun and that he's a little crazy because he got messed up fighting in Vietnam.

We watched Ben boost himself up on the hood. He fingertip-rolled the ball toward him until he could grab it. "Warm-up's over, people." The pavement rang under his sneakers as he jumped down. "Let's play!"

Like always, it was Girls versus Guys.

"Three against two!" Cody yelled. "We are *so* going to win."

Ben's dark bangs hung over his eyes as he bounced the ball from hand to hand. "The teams are Cass and Jemmie on Girls, me and Justin on Guys. Cody, you can fetch loose balls."

"Fetch?" Cody's shoulders drooped. "What do you think I am? A dog?"

I tried to cheer him up. "Hey, running loose balls is important."

"No it isn't! I wanna *play*, Ben." He bounced on his heels like he had to pee. "Please?"

I would've let Cody play—I have a big sister, and I know what it's like to be the little kid. Just a few months ago, Ben would've let him too.

3

But today, he just crossed his arms.

"You gotta let me!" Cody stamped a foot. "Mom's paying you to watch me!"

"And, oh boy, am I going to earn it," Ben muttered. "Listen, let's make a deal. You take another shot. Hit it and you're in. Miss and you run loose balls."

I knew what Cody would be doing one free throw from now. He never scores.

Considering his brother's offer, Cody grabbed the pole of the basketball hoop and swung himself around it.

Ben shook his head. "This is going to be one long, hot, boring, brother-bugged summer."

"Hey, summer's gonna be great!" I didn't want him to jinx it.

Cody held out his hands. "Sure, okay."

Ben tossed the ball. Cody whooped, surprised that he had caught it.

I reached for his shoulder as he trotted toward the chalked free-throw line. "Cody, you might want to"—he flung the ball—"aim." I watched it whump down on the carport roof.

The ball rolled to a stop in a pile of rotten leaves.

Justin rocked back on the worn-down heels of his kicks. "Good luck, Ben. You're gonna need a broom to reach that one."

Ben stared up at the ball, then turned and pointed down the street. "Go home, Cody. Now. And don't come back till you've had a couple more birthdays."

"B-but—" Cody sputtered. "I'm your paying summer job! Dad said!"

Ben's arm stayed straight out. "Only on weekdays."

"I didn't do it on purpose." Cody's face was getting all splotchy.

"Come on, Ben." I jogged over to Cody. "We know you didn't." I put a hand on his hot, damp shoulder. It felt trembly, like he was trying not to cry.

Ben walked over too, and dropped to one knee in front of him. "Give me a break, Cody. Go home. Bug Mom for a while. Let us get in a couple of games before school starts again."

Cody drooped away, kicking the curb every other step.

I latched on to Ben's T-shirt and swung him around. "You could've been a little nicer!" I whispered.

"I'm tired of being nice," he whispered back. "And I'm tired of getting balls off the roof. And I'm tired of the same old, same old." He looked around like the same old, same old included everything, even me. "I wish," he said, jamming his fists into the pockets of his cutoffs, "just for once, something exciting would happen around here."

This might just be the last summer of all of us together. Why couldn't he just enjoy it? "Be careful what you wish for," I warned.

He blew out, riffling his bangs. "Why? Wishes never come true anyway."

COdY

Cody stomped up the porch steps and shoved the front door open. "*Mo-om.* Ben's being mean!" He stomped into the kitchen. No Mom.

He opened the refrigerator, listened to the hum. Looked. Nothing good. As he closed the door, the postcard from his missing uncle—the card with the picture of the chicken platter on it—caught his eye. He wished he had a piece of fried chicken right now, but except for when Dad treated him and Ben to McDonald's or Kentucky Fried Chicken, his family was vegetarian.

He wandered into the living room, remembered Ben, and kicked the couch. Then he flopped down on his back on the floor and stared up at the ceiling fan.

The blades went around...and around...and around...

Joey Fowler, the kid in his class with the thick, bug-eye glasses, said that one time he stared at a fan so long without blinking, he hypnotized himself.

Around...and around... Cody's eyeballs were getting dry from not blinking, but he didn't feel hypnotized. Just sleepy.

He closed his eyes and smiled. The breeze from the fan felt good on his sweaty face. Something thumped in the closet on the other side of the room. "Aaaah!" Cody sprang to his knees. "Who's in there?"

Mom stuck her head out from behind the closet door. "Your mother."

"Why are you in the closet?"

"Sorting things out to go to Goodwill. Why are you not out with Ben and the gang?"

"Because..." Cody chewed on his bottom lip. "Because Ben *made* me come home."

"He did?" Mom walked over and sat down cross-legged in front of him. She tucked her flowery skirt under her bare feet and opened her arms. "Need a little lap time?"

He looked at her lap, but he was seven minus seven. Too old to climb onto a lap. He scooted closer so their knees touched. "Ben won't let me be on Guys."

Mom's long hair brushed his arm as she leaned toward him. "Maybe you should give him some space, Cody. Ben and his friends are about to start high school. You're a lot younger than they are."

"I'm almost seven!"

"Speaking of almost seven..." She pushed to her feet and padded to the bookcase. She picked up an envelope leaned against the row of family photo albums and a package wrapped in brown paper. "You got a birthday card, and a present. They came yesterday, but I forgot."

"But Mom, getting the mail is *my* job." Nobody let him do *anything* around here.

"I didn't *get* the mail. The mailman walked it up because of the package." She held the box out for him to see.

"Who's it from?"

"Aunt Sandy."

"Oh." He didn't even ask if he could shake it—Aunt Sandy gave Aunt Sandy presents, which meant it was something dumb. "What about the card?"

"I guess it's from one of your friends."

He didn't have any friends who sent cards, except valentines in the class valentine box.

The envelope she put in his hand looked like it had been run over a couple of times and there wasn't any return address. Cody didn't think people were allowed to send a letter without a return address, but it had gotten to him, Cody Paul Floyd.

He was going to open it, but he flipped it over first and saw writing on the back: *Do not open till your birthday, or monkeys will fly out your butt.* He looked up at Mom, shocked. "The B-word!"

Mom read the note over his shoulder. "It sounds like something that would come out of your brother's mouth, or Justin's." She took the card back and walked it and the Aunt Sandy package over to the stairs, where she set them on the bottom step—which meant he had to carry them up to his room the next time he went up. "Better forget the card until your birthday. You don't want monkeys to fly out of your B-word." She didn't have to tell him not to open the present.

Cody slumped, remembering. "Ben says I can't shoot hoops with them till I have *two* birthdays."

"*Two* birthdays? Well, we'd better find you something to do in the meantime. Why don't you help me go through the closet?" She held her hands out to him.

He slapped his hands into hers. "Okay."

Mom pulled him to his feet and led him across the room. She pointed to a heap on the floor. "This is the giveaway pile."

"Hey!" He swooped up the fuzzy brown thing on top of the stack. "My bear costume!"

"It doesn't fit you anymore. Let another kid get some use out of it."

He held the bear up to his chest. The feet dangled against his shins. "Oh, okay." The bear looked sad and crumpled when he dropped it back on top of Dad's old hockey skates.

"Check out the stuff on the closet floor." Mom shoved a step stool out of the way with one bare foot. "Board games. Go through them. I'll fix us a snack."

Cody knelt in the open closet door. Candy Land? Chutes and Ladders? Baby games. He didn't look through the whole stack. The smelly old games made his nose itch. Knee-walking, he shoved them over to the giveaway pile.

He glanced up. Hanging over the edge of the closet's high shelf were the floppy ears of one of the bunny mittens Aunt Sandy had knit for him. "You are *so* going to Goodwill!"

On tiptoes, he reached up and grabbed an ear. One good yank and the bunny came down, staring at him with blue button eyes. But he knew he needed both stupid bunny mittens for some other kid to get use out of, so he shoved the stool in close and climbed up.

All he could see was a stack of sweaters at the front of the shelf. He swept the pile off the shelf with his arm. Sweaters landed— *whump*—on the floor.

He reached farther and felt a crinkle. "Plastic bag." He grabbed a corner and yanked. "Ka-boom!" The bag of old magazines exploded on the floor.

When he reached again, his fingers touched something stiff— the bill of Ben's old Little League cap. He flicked the cap across the room. It sailed all the way to Dad's recliner and landed on the seat. "He shoots, he scores!"

Still no second bunny mitten. He patted his hand across the wooden shelf.

Felt empty.

The stool wobbled as he pushed up on his toes and reached way…way…way back. He was ready to give up when his fingers brushed against something too velvety to be a bunny mitten.

It made a *shhhh* sound as he inched it across the shelf. When he got it to the edge, a gray curve stuck out like a sliver of moon. "Hey, are you another hat?" He pulled it down. "Wow," he breathed.

The hat was the same browny gray as Elvis, his kindergarten class's pet gerbil. It felt the same too. Except it didn't shiver when he held it.

He plopped it on his head and—*whoosh*—the world disappeared.

Inside the hat smelled like G-dad's cough drops. The lining felt silky against his ears when he turned his head.

He heard Mom cross the living room. "Hey there, mystery man!"

The hat lifted and he smelled her clove perfume, then peanut butter.

"Ants on a log?" She held out a plate of peanut butter–stuffed celery sticks with raisins crawling on them.

He took the hat out of her hand and turned it over. "Dobbs," he read. The silver letters on the satin lining were perfect—like girl printing. "Who's Dobbs?"

"The manufacturer. Or"—Mom set the hat on his head carefully, so it balanced on his forehead—"you! You look like one of those old-time detectives."

He picked up a celery stick and crunched down on it, thinking. Dad only ever wore ball caps, except for that Santa hat when he thought Cody was too young to know he wasn't the *real* Santa. "Whose hat is this anyway?"

Mom's forehead wrinkled. "It's Uncle Paul's."

"For really?" Cody blinked. "Dad's brother? The one who disappeared?" He took another celery bite. "I'm seven minus seven and I never even met him."

"Actually, he lived with us for a while."

"Get out!" He jabbed his celery stick at her. "He lived with us?"

"Get out yourself!" She jabbed back with her celery stick. "He sure did. You were only three, probably too young to remember. The last we heard from him was that postcard on the refrigerator."

"The chicken platter?"

"The Space Needle. It's in Seattle. It just *looks* like a tray with a lid."

Long as Cody could remember, the postcard had never *not* been on the fridge. It was like it grew there. "We haven't heard from him for a long, long time."

"Not for a long, long, *long* time." Mom sighed.

Cody sort of remembered some photos from the family albums, but back then, Dad was just a chunky kid, his uncle a little skinny one.

"According to your dad, he was always restless and irresponsible, even as a kid. He just never took hold anywhere."

Cody had heard Dad tell Ben he had to "take hold" plenty of times. "Where's Uncle Paul now?"

"Who knows? Your uncle Paul is a wanderer."

"Maybe he'll wander back here."

"Really, Detective Dobbs?" She leaned in, touching her forehead to the brim of the hat. "Is that inside information?"

Cody played along. "Check. That means yes in detective talk."

"Good. Report back if you learn anything more."

"Check."

Ꮗ

With the closet sorted, Cody dug for a while out behind the tool-shed, looking for dinosaur bones. Ben had told him he could forget dinosaurs, except for the four junker cars parked in what Dad called his "dinosaur graveyard." But Cody was sure there were some real bones out there. Big ones. Digging with a bent trowel, he found a broken bottle and a baseball-size rock that would look better when he washed the dirt off. The hat watched from a lawn chair, staying clean.

11

But it got too hot to keep digging. And too boring. He wiped his hands on his shorts, picked up the hat, and went inside.

Mom was kneading bread, her long hair twisted back out of her face in a knot held with two chopsticks. "Want to punch the dough?" she asked.

"Nuh-uh. You can punch it. Want me to check on Ben?"

Mom glanced at the clock. "I guess you've given your brother enough of a break. But *watch* the game, okay? Fans are important too, you know."

Cody put on the hat and pushed the door open with one shoulder.

"Did you hear me, Detective Dobbs?" Mom called. "Don't crowd your brother."

"Check." Grabbing the brim so the hat would stay put, he jumped off the top porch step.

Cody walked down the driveway, keeping his head tipped back so the hat wouldn't slide. "Detective Dobbs was walking down the street," he said.

He stepped off the curb and—*foosh*—the hat slid down over his eyes.

It was pretty dark, but looking down, he could see his sneakers, one with the lace dragging.

He forgot the untied shoe when he saw a rock with sparkles in it next to the curb. He reached down and put the rock in his pocket.

Way down the street, a bouncing ball twanged against the road. Ben said that was "the call of the ball."

Cody followed the call, stepping one foot up on the curb and the other one down on the road. Up and down he walked like that, smelling cough drops and his own peanut-butter breath.

The ball was still calling, but now there was another noise too, like a dog scratching the door to come in. When he got close to it, the sound stopped.

Looking down, he saw worn leather sandals, dark feet with ashy toes, and the straws of a broom worn away on one side.

"Is this Cody Floyd I see walkin' blind down the road?" said a sandpapery voice.

"No."

"No? Then who we got under this big old go-to-work hat?"

The hat lifted. Light flooded in.

"Too bright!"

"It's called daylight—and it helps if you want to see where you're going." The skin around the eyes that stared into his crinkled in a smile.

"Hi, Nana Grace."

Jemmie's grandmother leaned the broom against her shoulder. The scratchy sound must've been her sweeping her driveway. "What you playing at, Cody, blindman's bluff?"

"I'm not Cody, I'm Detective Dobbs."

"Well now, Detective Dobbs." She put one hand on her bony hip, holding the hat with the other. "They got 'eye' in 'private eye' for a reason. To *be* one, you gotta be able to *see*."

Nana Grace brushed the top of the hat with her fingertips. "This hat is mighty fine, but the way you're wearin' it you're gonna get yourself killed." She shook her head. "I don't want to have to tell your mama you been hit by a car."

"I'm staying right at the edge. I'm being careful."

She pointed down. "While you're being careful, tie that shoe."

"Yes ma'am." He knelt on the hot road, pulled the lace tight, made the two loops, and knotted them. He stood up again. "May I have my hat back?"

Nana Grace bit her lip and squinted at him. "Bend your ears flat and hold 'em that way."

"Why?" But he bent his ears flat like she said. Nana Grace

grandmothered all the neighborhood kids. Everyone listened to her.

Using his ears the way Dad used shelf brackets, Nana Grace set the hat back on his head. She crossed her skinny arms and nodded once. "That'll work."

"Bye, Nana Grace." Now he could see, but his ears didn't like being shelf brackets. At the corner he eased the hat up to give them a break and they popped up straight.

He let the hat drop over his face again and followed the call of the ball.

JUStin

Ben scans his team—which no longer includes me. When Leroy showed up with his younger brother, Jahmal, they both refused to play on Girls. "Don't make me hurl, I ain't no girl," said Leroy, doing his idiot rapper rhyming thing.

So Jemmie pointed to me. "Come on, Big. You've been promoted to Girls."

I'll admit it, I got flustered—first because she noticed me specifically, and second because I sometimes think her nickname for me is code for "fat." When I didn't answer fast, she took it as a yes.

I've been a Girl now for, like, an hour, and I'm so hot I wish someone would kill me. Ben's sweating too. His hair is plastered to his face, but he doesn't notice. His head's in the game.

Deciding which of his two guys to hand off to, Ben holds the ball high. I'm white as school paste, but Ben's arms are tan from mowing lawns, almost as dark as Jemmie's. Being African American, she's tan year-round.

Jemmie gets all up in Ben's face, waving her arms. "You don't get points for hoggin' the ball, you know."

"Leroy!" Ben calls.

Of course, Leroy. Leroy's six foot fourteen and decked out in a blue satin basketball uniform like a pro—if a pro got his threads at Goodwill. But as he goes up for the catch, Jemmie cuts in front of him, snatches the ball, dribbles once as she pivots around him, then drives hard down the street.

I'm just thinking that being a Girl isn't half bad when Jemmie bounce-passes the ball to me. I reach, but it rolls off my fingertips.

Leroy lopes after the loose ball.

Cass snatches it on the run. She swings around, but when she jumps to take her shot, Ben steps right into her. She goes down so hard, her ponytail jolts straight out.

She hugs the ball and blinks up at him.

Geez. He knocked his girlfriend on her butt over a stupid ball?

"Foul!" Jemmie yells. "Free throw." She drags Cass to her feet.

Cass stands behind the chalk line we drew on the road. She's usually solid when it comes to free throws, but this time she misses. Guess being set down hard by Ben shook her up.

Leroy snags the ball as it rolls off the rim, then he sinks a turn-around jumper. He pumps his fist in the air, the rubber bracelets jiggling down his arm, and he grabs the ball. "Nothing but net!"

"What net? All we have is a rusty hoop." That's me talking—but not real loud.

Leroy rolls the ball down his arm and pops it in the air with his biceps. "It grows every hour, I got Leroy Power!"

Jemmie taps a foot. "Could you be any more in love with your-self?"

Hoping he keeps getting on her bad side with his showing off and the lame-o rhyming thing, I fade back to the safe zone, near the curb where the ball hardly ever goes, and watch Jemmie guard Leroy. He zigs, she zags—it's like they're dancing, they get so close.

Ben says on a scale of one to ten, one being "not a chance" and ten being "done deal," getting Jemmie to like me is a high three. But as my best friend, sometimes he overestimates.

Leroy bumps Jemmie with his shoulder. She bumps back.

I'd put my chances with her at negative fourteen. Leroy has blue eyes like you never see on a black guy, and no zits—while I have one on my chin that deserves its own zip code. Leroy's all slick moves, and here I am hiding out at the curb, my hands in the pockets of my plaid shorts.

I mean, who shoots hoops with their hands in their pockets?

Who wears plaid shorts?

"Give it!" Jemmie's gold hoop earrings flash as she slaps at the ball. To Jemmie, life is a contact sport. To me, it's more like a rerun of a bad old TV show—without snacks.

Leroy twists, keeping the ball away from her. "The girl can't steal, 'cause I'm the real deal!"

I sit down on the curb. This time Jemmie's glare is for me, but it's stinkin' hot, and I'm not really in the game anyway.

Leroy passes to his kid brother—and Jahmal scores. Jahmal. A kid not much older than Cody.

෧෧

Girls is ahead by eighteen points when a little kid comes poking down the road wearing a Humphrey Bogart fedora. (If you don't know about HB or fedoras, you probably don't watch old movies with your mom.) Everyone else is too busy grunting and sweating to notice him as he bumps along the curb.

I shade my eyes. "Cody?" The hat covers his whole head and makes the scrawny neck sticking out of it look like a pencil. "Can you see where you're going?"

"I can see the ground." He stops. "And what makes you think I'm Cody?"

"I recognize the shoes."

"And the T-shirt." Ben rests his palms on his thighs, gasping. "Which used to be mine."

"Doesn't prove it," Cody says.

17

Leroy revs up. "Oh, you can't disguise, 'cause I reck-o-nize your skinny little thighs." He bounces the ball, swatting it from one hand to the other. "You *are* Cody."

"Am not."

Leroy spins the ball on one finger. "Who are you, then?"

"Dobbs."

Leroy tosses the ball up in the air. Still spinning, it lands on his finger again. "Nice to meet you, Mr. Dobbs."

"*Detective* Dobbs."

I like the hat. I'd wear it to high school next fall if it was mine. It would make me either cool or weird. "Where'd you get the hat, Detective Dobbs?" I ask.

"Closet."

Leroy dribbles a fast circle around Cody. "Detect this, *Detective* Dobbs." He pops the ball straight at Cody's chest.

Cody can barely catch a ball when he's looking right at it—but this time his hands whip up and he grabs it.

"Hey! You saw that coming!" says Leroy.

"Nuh-uh! I *felt* it. I have new detection powers."

"For real? Let's see if you can feel that ball into the basket, Mr. Detection Powers," Leroy says.

Cody holds the ball in both hands and turns slowly.

"That's it, that's it," Leroy coaxes as Cody turns away from the hoop.

"Leroy?" Jemmie pops him on the shoulder with her fist. "Quit being a butt."

"Not tryin' to be rude, just messin' with the dude."

"Is anyone else getting tired of shooting hoops with Dr. Seuss?" I ask.

Leroy points to Cody. "And the Cat in the Hat."

Which I have to admit is a decent comeback.

Leroy snaps the elastic waist of his satin shorts and struts over to Cody. "Let me help you out there, Detective Dobbs." But halfway to Cody he stops and rests his knuckles on his hips.

Like a compass needle finding north, Cody is slowly turning toward the basket. When the basket is dead ahead, he plants his feet wide and swings the ball back and forth between his legs.

Leroy blows out his breath. "You still have that broom handy, Ben?"

If this was a movie, Cody would nail it and everyone would cheer, but it isn't. It's just life.

"Take your time, Cody," I say under my breath as he swings the ball between his skinny legs. Not a chance he'll hit the hoop, but why not stretch the moment when it still seems possible?

"Hey, bop-a-loo-bop!" After one last crazy swing, the ball flies.

Jemmie lets out a whoop. Cass does a perky cheerleader jump. Ben slaps Cody's shoulder. Jahmal gapes, like he won't believe what just happened unless he sees the instant replay.

"Nothing but net!" I pump my fist in the air. Luckily no one notices the move.

Leroy's so impressed, he forgets to rhyme. "You da man, little dude!"

Detective Dobbs pushes the hat up and sees everyone celebrating, then grins. "Told you. I have powers!"

Leroy runs the ball down, then shoves it into Cody's hands. "Again!" He jams the hat down on Cody's head, then leans over and looks up under the brim. "You sure you can't see?"

"Just the ground." Leaving out the "hey, bop-a-loo-bop," Cody flings the ball two-handed over his head and puts it through the hoop a second time.

We all go wild.

Leroy scoops up the ball. "Let's see you go three for three."

Don't try it, I coach Cody silently. Three for three? Nothing that sweet ever happens.

I guess Cody knows it too. He ambles toward the curb. "The hat says maybe later."

"Let *me* take a shot wearing it." Leroy snatches the hat.

"Hey!" Cody throws his arms over his bare head. "Give it back!"

"One shot to see what it's got."

"The power only works for the hat-finder—and that's me."

Leroy trots back, cocks the hat so it covers his eyes, and shoots, but it goes long and…*splat*, it's back in the rotten leaves on Mr. B's carport roof.

"Told you," says Cody, staring up at the ball.

Leroy shrugs. "Don't need that old hat anyway. Hooping in a hat ain't where it's at."

Leroy starts basketball camp—and summer school—on Monday. The first because he's so good, and the other because he's so bad. I just hope he'll be too busy to hang out with us.

Without bothering to get permission, he scrambles up onto the truck hood and long-arms the ball. He jumps down, plops the hat on Cody's head, and pushes the ball into the kid's chest. "Come on. Show me that hat trick one more time."

But Ben hangs an arm around his brother's shoulders. "You getting hungry, Detective Dobbs?" Ben asks.

The hat nods.

"Me too. Let's go check out what Mom's doing with tofu and sprouts today."

Cody skips backwards a step and says, "See you guys!"

"Sure you don't want to join Girls?" I call after him.

He stops. "Can I?"

"No." Ben turns him toward home. "Catch you guys later."

In the split second it takes Ben to look back and wave at us, Cody runs smack into a recycling bin.

Ben slaps the hat brim. "Take off the stupid hat." When Cody doesn't, Ben puts a hand on his shoulder.

"Bye, Ben!" Cass leans toward him like he's magnetic. He lifts a hand, but doesn't turn around.

If I had a girlfriend I would turn around. Heck, I'd walk backwards until she disappeared over the horizon. I glance at Jemmie, but she's taking free throws, nailing them one after another. That girl doesn't need a magic hat.

I sure could use one, though.

ben

I told my brother to take the hat off, but he acted like the hat made him deaf on top of blind. Cody always overdoes things. When our grandfather taught him pig latin, I was "En-bay" for weeks. Now it was the hat.

After he smacked into Ms. Dupree's recycling bin, I kept a hand on his shoulder.

"Hey, Ben? You know whose hat this is?" He did a skip-step to keep up. "It's Uncle Paul's, the one who disappeared!"

In Cody's head I bet our uncle disappeared in a puff of smoke. "Uncle Paul didn't disappear. He's traveling."

"He's only sent one postcard since I was three years old. That's pretty disappeared."

Yeah, it was. Sometimes I still missed my uncle. He was way cooler than his older brother, my dad. I steered my own brother away from the curb. "I'd like to pull an Uncle Paul sometime. Travel around. See things."

"Can I come?"

"No." I gave his shoulder a squeeze. "But don't worry. I'll send you more than one postcard."

"How many?"

"Two."

Cody twisted toward me. "Two?"

"Doof."

"You're kidding?"

Since he couldn't see my face, I gave his shoulder another squeeze.

"Does one squeeze mean yes?"

I squeezed again.

"So, one is yes, and two is no. And three can be maybe?"

There's a reason I call Cody my little "bother." I gave his shoulder three hard squeezes, then changed the subject. "Hey, that was pretty sweet the way you made those shots. You could you see the hoop, right?"

"No way."

I pushed up on the hat brim. As soon as his eyes came into view he smiled, showing off his half-grown-in big front teeth—he really believes the tooth fairy is keeping the ones he lost in a "special place."

"Whoa!" Cody slapped the sunflower Mom painted on our mailbox. "We're already home!" He flapped the mailbox door open and shut.

"You didn't even check."

"Of course not. It's Sunday."

"Then why'd you open the box?"

"For luck."

"That's how you made those hoops, right? Luck?"

Cody blinked up at me. "I dunno. I've only ever made a few baskets in my whole entire life. Today, without even looking, I just let go of the ball and—*swish!*" He stared at his hands. "When I held it, there was this…like…tingle."

Oh boy, here we go. "Tingle?"

"You know…sort of a…magic tingle." Cody opened and closed his hands, staring at them.

I crossed my arms. "A *magic* tingle?"

"Yes, a magic tingle!" Cody nodded so hard, the hat slid back over his eyes.

I walked away. "I'm going in for lunch." He could find his own way up the driveway, or maybe the hat would tingle him in the right direction.

"Why couldn't it be magic?" he shouted.

I sighed and walked back. "Magic is a little-kid thing, Cody." I took the hat off his head. "Time to get over it. You're about to turn seven."

But with my uncle's hat in my hands I felt a different kind of tingle. With his hat in my hands I started remembering him. No poof of smoke, but Uncle Paul *had* disappeared. One day he was here, sleeping in the room where Cody slept now; the next day he was gone.

"Say, Ben, is seven years old when you forget magic is real?" Even Cody's freckles seemed to be staring up at me.

"No. Seven is when you figure out that it never was real."

"Oh."

"Don't feel bad. It's kind of a good thing that magic is fake. Even in stories it's only nice at first. It always messes up the person who has it."

"Nuh-uh! Not Cinderella! Cinderella married the prince!"

"And they lived boringly ever after."

Cody blinked up at me. "But the hat gave me powers!"

"Like the powers you had the time you tied your blanket around your shoulders and 'flew' off the top of the monkey bars?" I didn't mention the broken collarbone. I'd tried the flying thing myself on the swings with Cass, both of us jumping when our swings hit the top. I got scraped up bad and her swing smacked her in the back of the head. Every kid has powers, until they try to use them.

"That was different. The blanket wasn't magic."

"Get real, Cody. 'Magic' only works in those comic books you like."

"Not comics. Manga!"

"I'm telling you, just be glad hat magic isn't real. If it was, and you messed up? You could destroy the planet." I jogged across the yard. "Come on, Cody, let's eat."

"Gimme back my magic hat!"

I loped up the porch steps and winged the hat at him, didn't even aim. Still, it landed on his head.

"See?" he whooped, pushing it back. "The hat likes me. It came right to me! Good old hat."

"Hats don't like people, and hitting that hoop was luck, not magic. You can wear the hat, but you're still gonna have a normal, boring summer—and your head's gonna sweat."

Cody took the hat off and stared down at it. "*I* know you're magic," he mumbled. "But if I mess up, don't destroy the planet, okay?"

jemmie

All sweaty, I pumped the front of my T-shirt to let in some air. "Wanna go now, Cass?" Girls had won three games out of four and my stomach was talking to me, big-time.

Cass finished tying her sneaker and straightened up. "Sure."

"Hey, Jemmie." Leroy's voice came from behind us.

I turned. "Hey, what?"

His arms hung at his sides, the ball tucked against his waist like it was part of him. "How about some fun with a little one-on-one?"

The girls at school called him "Lookin' Good Leroy," and he did, but I got to look at him more than they did. Listen to him too.

He glanced at the ball, then back at me. "Unless you're 'fraid you can't make the grade."

"You *know* I'm not afraid, but I *am* hot and hungry. I'll whup you some other day. Ask Big to play."

Slumped on the curb, Big looked like something put out for trash pick-up.

"Nah," said Leroy. "The man can't hoop."

"Me!" His kid brother Jahmal slapped at the ball. "I can hoop 'cause I got the poop!"

"Stupid must be contagious," Big mumbled.

"Let's go." I grabbed Cass by her pocket, then turned back.

"Piano lesson tomorrow, Big?" He practices at my house. We have a piano and he doesn't.

"Yup. Monday, same as always." He sighed just like I would if I was thinking about *my* piano lesson—only *I* would mean it. Guess he was trying to sound cool about the lesson so Leroy wouldn't make some stupid rhyme about a kid who'd rather play piano than shoot hoops.

"See ya later, Big!" I yelled. I knew my "See ya later" would give Lookin' Good Leroy something to think about.

෨෯

"Jemmie, that you?" my grandmother called as we ran up the steps of my house.

I opened the front door. "Me and Cass, Nana." We fell into the cool.

In the kitchen, Nana Grace was mixing up a big bowl of potato salad, hugging it against the front of her flowered apron. "You two are right on time." Bread and sliced baloney were already on the table where my little brother Artie sat coloring. "Somebody put out dishes."

Cass swung open the cupboard door. "Can you believe Cody hit two shots with that hat over his eyes?"

I stood at the sink and filled the water glasses, then let the water run cold over my wrists. "He got lucky, I guess."

"Lucky? Twice?" Cass set the dishes on the table and did a hocus-pocus thing with her hands. "Maybe it was the magic of the hat!"

My grandmother handed Artie a cracker as she passed his chair. "What're you talking about, Cass?"

"Cody has this hat he says gives him powers."

27

"Oh, the hat." My grandmother smiled and shook her head. "I just hope he don't get himself run over with that magic hat down over his eyes."

Cass walked to the table with a fistful of silverware. "Too bad there's no such thing as a magic hat. I'd use it to make this summer last forever."

"Good thing you *don't* have a magic hat!" I said, carrying the water glasses over from the sink. "I'm ready for something new. Besides, there's no such thing as magic, and definitely no such thing as a magic hat—unless your name is Harry Potter."

Nana set the potato salad bowl down with a thump. "Why not a magic hat? Magic can come from all kinds of strange places."

I turned toward my grandmother. "You don't believe in magic, do you, Nana?"

"Doesn't matter what *I* believe. Question is, what does Cody Floyd believe?"

Cass sat down at the table. "He definitely believes in the power of the hat." She pulled her legs up and hugged her knees, her heels hooked over the edge of the chair seat. "But you know, Cody *never* hits the hoop, even when he's looking right at it. Maybe it *was* the hat."

I took the blue crayon out of Artie's hand and gave him a red. "No such thing as blue apples, Smarty Artie." I turned to Cass. "And there's no such thing as magic hats or magic anything. And why would you want summer to last forever anyway?"

Nana's cool fingers brushed against my hot neck. "Don't go hard on Cass. Nothing wrong with liking things as is, and don't go hard on Cody, either. Everybody needs some kind of magic to get 'em through."

As we grabbed hands and asked the blessing, I thought about Leroy and his rapping. Maybe talking big was Leroy's magic hat— talking big and jamming the ball through the hoop. With no dad at home, his mom called him "the man of the house." He had a lot on his shoulders. He never would've been able to go to basketball camp this summer if it cost money. And even the fact that it was free wouldn't have helped if his aunt hadn't lost her job. Now she'd be watching Jahmal so Leroy didn't have to.

Nana put her hands on her tired back and straightened up. "Big's got a lesson tomorrow. If that boy's coming over to practice later, I'd best put together a sandwich for him. He's always hungry."

"Sure." I squirted mustard on my bread. "He said he'd be over." Big's magic hat was his music, definitely.

I don't know what it would be for Cass. Maybe running, maybe hanging on to the same old, same old.

Running's *my* magic hat, for sure. Something bothers me? I run.

My father died of cancer a couple of years ago. Most of the time I can outrun thinking about it.

But sometimes, when Big is playing my father's old piano I sit at the bend in the stairs where he can't see me and I pretend I'm listening to my father play.

I wish Dad could've heard him. He would've said, "Mmmm, mmmm. That boy's got blue-eyed soul."

ben

We'd shot hoops and eaten lunch. After scarfing down his tofu burger, Cody had wandered off while I cleaned up. I wiped the table, then rested my back against the fridge.

Now what? The first week in August my family would be camping in the North Georgia mountains, but until then? Not much.

I had a stack of required summer reading to do before I hit AP English at Leon High. Dad had recommended I "pace myself," which meant don't wait until the end of August to start reading, but even he would be amazed. I'd started reading *To Kill a Mockingbird* first thing this morning, and until the day cooled down a little I couldn't think of anything else to do.

I wandered into the den where I'd left the book open on the arm of the sofa, but somebody had closed it. "Cody!" I yelled. No answer. Some teacher had told him that leaving an open book facedown hurt its spine. Cody thinks a book's spine actually hurts—he isn't real clear on the difference between living things and just things.

I flopped down, shoving the couch back a few inches, and it made a funny sound—like a surprised snort. A snorting couch? I was beginning to think like Cody.

It wasn't hard to find my place in the book. I hadn't gotten far. Page four—so maybe I didn't need to kill him.

I was a couple of chapters in when I heard a knock on the front door, then the sound of the door opening slowly. "Ben?"

"In here!" I yelled.

Justin appeared in the door, a fresh ketchup stain on his Killer App T-shirt.

"Fries for lunch?"

"Nope. I finished the fries at breakfast." He looked down. "The foraging was slim so I had cereal. Since it was lunch I thought I'd try Special K with ketchup. FYI? Bad idea." The couch made the same funny sound as Jus fell onto the cushions beside me. He didn't mention it, so I didn't either. He nodded at the book in my lap. "What're you reading?"

"Something on the list."

"Come on, we just got out of school and you're doing required reading?" He drummed on the edge of the couch.

"Anything going on at your place?" I asked.

"Just the Mom and Dad show. Dad's home this week. He and Mom are having 'together time.'"

"How's that working out?"

"About like you'd expect. Hey, you think Cody would lend me his power hat so I can kick Dad's butt out?"

I stretched and hung the book back over the arm of the couch. "There's *gotta* be something to do."

Justin shoved his legs out straight. "Not necessarily." His socks ballooned around his ankles; they'd lost their snap.

We rested our necks on the back of the couch and stared at the ceiling.

I was about to ask him if the swirl in the plaster over our heads looked like a dog sniffing its own butt when a high-pitched voice from behind the couch yelled, "She's coming!"

I whipped around. "Cody, you little punk! Why didn't you say you were back there?"

"I would've, but you were mad about the book."

"Who's coming?" Justin asked.

"Cass!"

I peered into the gap between the couch and the wall. No wonder he'd made those noises. We had him pinned good, the brim of his hat folded up on both sides. I snatched the hat off his head. "Who says she is?"

"Why should I tell you?" He blinked up at me. "You don't believe in it."

"Hey!" The couch creaked as Justin leaned forward. "Check it out, Ben."

I turned and looked out our front window. Cass was wandering slowly down the street.

Cody crawled out from behind the couch. "Told ya!" he crowed.

"Lucky guess, Detective Dobbs."

"It wasn't lucky, and it wasn't a guess. Can I please have my hat?"

I plopped it back on his head and watched Cass, who had leaned over to smell one of Mom's roses. Her parents don't like her knocking on our door—something about chasing boys.

"She wants you to notice her," said the voice under the hat.

"Okay, Ben." Justin shoved himself to his feet. "Guess you better go out there and notice her. And I better get over to the Lewises' and practice."

I pointed at the ketchup on his shirt. "You might want to rinse that off before Jemmie sees you."

He held out the front of his shirt and shrugged. "Like it'll make a difference."

"Wash it off," said the voice from under the hat.

CODY

He could see Ben outside, talking to Cass by the bush with the creamsicle orange roses. Cass had one skinny leg twisted around the other. Ben wore a stupid grin.

Justin had already scuffed down the road with a big wet spot on his shirt.

Cody flumped down on the couch. He needed to think, but there was that book, open again. He hesitated, then closed the book about killing birds.

What had just happened? It was like one second he wasn't even thinking and the next second—*tingle!*—he'd opened his mouth and blurted out, "She's coming!" He opened and closed his mouth now to see if the hat would make him talk again, but it didn't.

Dad always said there was a logical explanation for everything. Maybe Uncle Paul, who was a real person, not a hat, was behind the tingly messages.

That would be sort of logical.

Cody pushed the hat back on his forehead and walked into the kitchen.

The refrigerator hummed hello, but he wasn't looking for a snack. Instead, he studied the picture on the front of the postcard stuck to the refrigerator door with a smiley magnet. It *still* looked like a platter with a lid—and for sure fried chicken underneath.

"Detective Dobbs," he whispered. A good detective wouldn't be distracted by a platter of fried chicken.

When he tugged on it, the smiley magnet fell and rolled under the refrigerator. But the postcard stayed where it was. Stuck. He had to peel it off. It'd been hanging there so long, it was used to the spot.

When he turned it over, the message on the back was in pencil. Faded bad. The handwriting? Seemed as if he'd seen it before—but lots of people wrote sloppy.

He struggled to read the words. "Some…good stuff…happening out…here." The letters slanted back. Maybe his uncle was left-handed like him. "Think I'm…finally on the…right track! More details soon."

In the very bottom corner it said, "Hang in there, Shotgun!"

"Who's Shotgun?" Cody whispered. "And how come you never sent the details?"

He shoved the postcard under the hatband, put the hat on, and opened the fridge. He had to think, but he needed a snack first.

"Most moms wouldn't let a kid wear a hat inside the house," Mom said when she walked into the kitchen. But she didn't make him take it off.

ꙮ

"All right, Cody," she said as she cooked supper. "*No* moms would let a son wear that hat at the dinner table. Put it back in the closet before Dad gets home."

Instead he snuck it up the stairs to his room—no hats at the table, that was the main thing. He hung it on one of the carved pineapple bedposts—his bed had been Mom's when she was a kid.

"Wait here," he told the hat.

Dad came home, took off his coveralls, and scrubbed the grease off his arms at the kitchen sink. They ate supper. Watched TV.

The hat was waiting for Cody when he went up to bed. "Hi, hat."

He pulled off his shirt and practiced a superhero pose in the mirror. "Wait!" He put on the hat carefully and did it again. "Super detective!" He sucked his stomach in until his ribs stuck out.

Suddenly, he was sure his uncle was skinny too. Not regular skinny, but skinny-bone-skinny. Totally not like Dad, the Big Beluga.

Was the hat showing him his uncle, or was he remembering stuff from before he was three years old? Seemed like the uncle in his head was walking down their driveway get-out-of-here fast, and someone was yelling at him.

Cody opened his eyes in the dark of the hat, his heart pounding.

He took the hat off, put on his pj's, and dove into bed.

He was still seeing the uncle in his head when a voice boomed, "Good night, Sport!"

"Aaaah!" Cody sat straight up in bed.

Dad filled the door. "Didn't mean to scare you." He drummed his palms on the door frame, then stopped. Looking at the hat, he sighed. "Look what you've got." He came into the room and lifted the hat off the bedpost.

Cody pulled his knees up so Dad would sit, but he didn't. "That's Uncle Paul's hat."

"Yup." Dad turned the hat in his hands. "I see you have the postcard too. Be careful with it, okay? It's all we've got, at least till he sends another one."

"I will."

Dad knuckle-rubbed the top of Cody's head. "You two share a birthday, you know."

"And a name. Only backwards." Cody pointed at his own chest—"Cody Paul"—then at the hat—"Paul Cody. We're exact opposites."

Dad shook his head. "Thank God for that. Two Paul Codys in one family? Disaster."

Cody rested his chin on his knees. "Is Uncle Paul left-handed, like me?"

"Sure is." Dad gazed at the loaded shelf over Cody's bed. "And you both like comic books."

"Manga!"

Dad turned the hat in his hands. "Your uncle picked this up at the Goodwill on Mabry, wore it to a job interview I got for him." One corner of his mouth perked up in a sort-of smile. "I could've killed him. Who hires a long-haired guy in a Goodwill hat?"

"He didn't get the job, huh?"

"Believe it or not, he did. He lasted two whole days, then hit the road."

The image of his skinny uncle walking fast down the driveway flashed in Cody's head. Was Dad the one doing the yelling?

Dad pulled the postcard from the hatband and read the scribbled writing: "...finally on the right track." The bedsprings chirped as Dad sat down. "You wouldn't know the right track if it bit you." Now Dad was talking to the hat too. "I tried so hard to keep you out of trouble."

"Like Ben keeps me out of trouble?"

Dad snorted. "With you two it'll be the other way around."

"Ben's responsible."

"Like when he almost got both of you killed over Christmas break?"

"He wasn't *trying* to get us killed. The boat just ran out of gas and it got dark and the wind was blowing the wrong direction."

Dad shook his head. "Sometimes I wonder if having Ben watch you this summer is a good idea."

"Yeah, I can pretty much take care of myself."

Dad slapped his knees. "Question is, who'll look out for Ben?"

"Me! I will."

"All right!" Dad gave Cody a quick hug, then stood. "You're in charge." He jammed the card back into the hatband and tossed the hat at the bedpost. It caught, spun, and then wobbled to a stop. "Check in, Paulie," Dad said, pointing at the hat. He turned off the light and left the door open a crack like always, so light from the hall could sneak in.

Cody lay back. What if Ben disappeared like Uncle Paul? Ben always said he wanted to go someplace.

Cody turned and knocked on the wall, *thump, thump*. Two knocks was how the brothers said good night, and how Cody got Ben's attention when he had a nightmare. Ben wasn't in bed yet; Cody could hear him in his room, messing around.

Ben didn't thump back.

Cody knocked again, louder.

"Aren't you getting a little old for this?" Ben called.

"I'm only six."

"For seven—make that six—more days." Ben knocked twice. "Go to sleep now, little bro."

Cody flopped onto his back and looked up. A giant vampire bat was swooping across the ceiling!

He almost yelled. Good thing he didn't. It was just a hat shadow from the light coming in from the hall.

But it *looked* like a bat.

He knocked softly, one last time.

"We already did that!" Ben called.

"Just double-checking!" Cody closed his eyes.

The bat on the ceiling hovered over him all night long.

monday
(seven minus six)

Justin

That thing about putting the pillow over your head so you can't hear? Doesn't work. The battle going on in my parents' room buzz-saws right through the flimsy bag of feathers.

The clock by my bed says 4:27 when I pull on my clothes and sneak out.

Not that I need to sneak. The parental units are too busy fighting to notice me creeping past their door, down the creaky stairs, across the messy living room, through the kitchen where a week's worth of dishes are piled in the sink, and out into the dark.

I can still hear them shouting as I cut across the damp grass. Our neighbor's light is on. Must be fun living next door to us.

On my way to Ben's I pass a cat sleeping on the hood of a car. A couple of porch lights are on, but the houses are dark. Everyone's asleep but my family—and our next-door neighbors.

I need to crash at the Floyds', but getting inside is going to be tricky.

When I reach Ben's driveway I stand there awhile, looking up. There's Ben's window. No light on. He's asleep—like I'd be, if my parents didn't fight all night.

I grab a handful of gravel and toss it toward the window. It splats against the side of the house. I try again and hear it clatter against the glass.

I hold my breath but the light doesn't come on. I'm picking up another handful of pebbles when the window opens. "Jus?" Ben sounds hoarse, like somebody just woke him up from a deep sleep.

"Who else?"

"Wait there." The window scrapes closed again.

Sneaking down the stairs takes time in a house where people don't yell all night. I watch moths ping against the bulb of the porch light.

The door opens. He's wearing boxers and an old T-shirt. "Sorry," I whisper as I slide inside.

"I was awake anyway, thinking."

"About what?"

"About how my uncle Paul used to hitchhike to Panama City Beach when he was in high school."

"Why were you thinking about that?"

He turns on the little light over the stove and leans against the oven door—even in the dim light I can see that the kitchen is clean, no yesterday dishes anywhere. "Do you ever have the feeling all the cool stuff happened before we got old enough to do any of it?" he asks.

"Like hitching to the coast? Does anyone even hitch anymore?"

"That's what I'm talking about!" He stares into the dark outside the kitchen window.

"I'd be up for it." I pull out a chair and sit. "My folks wouldn't even notice. But yours? Double heart attack. Plus, nobody hitch-hikes anymore except mass murderers."

Frustrated, he shakes his head. "When it comes to having a cool summer, we're toast." He gets a bag of coffee out of the freezer, then glances at me over his shoulder. "Your T-shirt's inside out."

I hold out the front of the shirt and look down, then shrug. "I wore it right side out yesterday." At my house the score is dirty shirts, ten; clean shirts, zero. Still, inside out? I have *some* standards.

I skin the shirt off and put it on right. "I dressed kind of fast," I say, popping my head out the neck hole. I glance down, and there's the ghost of yesterday's ketchup stain. In better light, I bet you could see sweat stains too.

"They get up this early to fight?" Ben whispers, filling the coffee pot at the sink.

"What do you mean, get up? They've been at it all night."

The only time it was peaceful at my house was for a couple of months when Dad left. Then he came back. I rub my burning eyes.

Ben makes an extra-big pot of coffee. He pours a mug for each of us, then sets the squeeze-top honey bear on the table. I squirt long drizzles into both cups. Ben sloshes in some milk.

We sit with our elbows on the table. Upstairs, a toilet flushes.

Mr. Floyd comes down in his boxers too, but no T-shirt. He stops scratching his hairy belly when he sees me. "Justin?" He stares at me like I'm the answer to the question, "What's wrong with this picture?"

"Hi, Mr. Floyd. Good morning?"

"Did you spend the night?"

"No, sir. I just got here."

He checks out the clock on the stove. "Do your parents know where you are?"

"Where else would I be?"

Mr. Floyd crosses his arms. "You better call them."

"I don't think they'd hear the phone."

Ben takes another mug out of the cupboard. "Coffee, Dad?"

"And newspaper?" I ask. I go out to the box and bring in the *Democrat*, figuring Ben will explain. As I come back in with the paper, Mr. Floyd lifts a cast-iron skillet off a hook on the wall.

We're about to dig in to hash browns and a cheese omelet when Ben's mom scuffs down the stairs in a purple robe. Staring, she does a repeat of "What's wrong with this picture?"

42

Mrs. Floyd thinks I should call home, too, then zeroes in on our heaped plates. We aren't breaking any of her vegetarian rules, but she's a big believer in fiber. Breakfast, according to Ben's mom, should be like gnawing a chair leg.

"Comfort food," Mr. Floyd whispers.

"Oh, honey." Ben's mom puts a hand on my back and rubs. "You look so tired." She watches me eat until I clean the plate, then drapes an arm around my shoulders. "Come with me."

I let her walk me to the sofa. "Lie down."

Roll over... Beg... Sometimes I wish the snarky little guy in my head who turns everything into a joke would take a break.

I lie down and Mrs. Floyd shakes out the fuzzy pink blanket that hangs on the back of the sofa. It's summer and plenty warm, but it's the thought that counts. "I'm okay," I mutter as the blanket settles.

I pass out fast, but it isn't a deep sleep.

The front door opens and closes a couple of times as Mrs. Floyd takes off for the utilities office and Mr. Floyd heads for Baker's Garage, his summer job until he goes back to being a high school auto mechanics teacher.

I open an eye and Ben is in the nearby recliner, zonked. The house is so quiet, I can hear the clock ticking on the book shelf. I count it off in 4/4 time until I drift...

I'm asleep for real when I feel someone sit down on my chest.

We both yell, and I bolt up so fast I dump Cody on his butt. The hat that kept him from seeing me pops off and rolls on its brim until it hits the bookcase.

Ben, stretching his arms over his head, yawns so big I can see his back teeth. It's daylight out.

Cody crawls over to the bookcase. "You okay, hat?" Up on his knees, he brushes off some imaginary dust.

"FYI, Jus?" Ben snaps the footrest on the recliner down. "You drool in your sleep."

"How would you know? You were asleep too."

"Not the whole time. Trust me, you drool."

"Great!" I flop back on the couch. "I can't even sleep right."

"So," Ben says. "What do you wanna do today?"

Nothing much comes to mind. "Eat a big bowl of ice cream?"

"No," Cody blurts out. "We're not allowed!"

"He was kidding," Ben says.

"Oh." Cody looks sad that he didn't get the joke.

"Hey," I say. "Isn't today seven minus six?"

"Yeah," says Ben. "I think I saw something about that in today's paper. Happy seven minus six. How about if *you* pick out what we do today, little bro?"

My buddy must be desperate if he's asking Cody for ideas.

"Me? Choose?" Cody looks proud—then worried. "Just a second." Cody puts the hat on and lets it drop over his face. He sits like that for a minute. "The hat says we should go for a walk."

"A walk?" Ben doesn't sound thrilled.

"The hat says seven minus six is a good day to look for something."

Ben rests his forearms on his thighs, leans toward his brother, and nudges the hat back. "What kind of something?"

"I dunno. The hat'll show us."

"I'm up for it." I toss back the pink blanket. "I gotta stay busy and out of the house for the next"—I pretend to study the clock on the bookshelf—"two and a half months."

"Okay, Detective." Ben thumps the top of the hat with a knuckle. "Find us something."

"Check!" says the kid in the hat, throwing his shoulders back.

jemmie

Cass and me were still in our pajamas when Nana Grace leaned forward in her chair by the window. "Here they come again! Lord, Cody can't see a thing with that hat over his face, and he's leading them other two around."

The first time they went by, Ben had his hands on his brother's shoulders, Big walking right behind them. When Cody tripped, they piled into each other.

This time they stopped. Ben dropped to one knee to talk to Cody, who was still under the hat.

The hat kind of wobbled. It looked like Cody was shaking his head no. Then Ben shrugged at Big and put his hands back on Cody's shoulders. They started walking again. I figured it was some kind of game. I went out on the porch and leaned toward them over the railing. "Hey! What're you doing?"

"We're on a hat expedition!" Big yelled back. "Cody's idea."

"Nuh-uh!" Cody shouted. "It was the hat's idea!"

I stuck my head back in the door. "Cass? Wanna go on a hat expedition?"

"Come in here right this second and get decent!" my grandmother ordered.

I turned back to the guys and held out my arms. "I *am* decent, right?"

Big gulped. "Are those your pajamas?" He turned red.

"Well, yeah." I felt *my* face get hot—but I didn't know why. My pj's were a pink tank top and baggy flannel bottoms with fairies on them. No matter what my grandmother said or how red-faced Big got, I was decent!

"Back in a minute!" I rushed inside.

☉☉

The guys were sitting on the steps when we came out. Big looked away. I wanted to punch his arm and say, Hey, now that I'm wearing shorts, flip-flops, and a T-shirt, I'm showing you way more skin than I did in my pajamas. But then I thought about seeing *him* in *his* pajamas and I looked away too. Must be something about the word "pajamas."

We started walking, all of us trailing along behind Cody.

"What's a hat expedition?" Cass dragged her fingers through her hair—we dressed so fast, she hadn't had time to brush.

Justin tapped on the top of the hat. "Explain, O Cody of the Third Eye."

"The hat is leading us."

"Leading us where?" I asked.

"In circles," said Ben.

I glanced at Big. He had no business making comments about anything *I* wore. "Say, Big? Isn't that the same shirt you had on yesterday?"

"Uh, no. I have two like this."

Who had two T-shirts that have "Killer App" and a robot-looking guy with a sword on the front? One was too many, and the pinkish stain looked familiar. But for once I didn't run my mouth. Nana Grace leaves stacks of neatly folded laundry on my bed. I've never

46

been inside Big's house, but I bet no one leaves *him* stacks of clean laundry.

For the next while we followed Cody…and sweated.

Finally, Ben pulled back on his brother's shoulders. "Running out of neighborhood."

"But we're not *there* yet," the hat whined.

"Come on, Cody." Ben leaned down. "Let's go home, put the hat in the closet, and—"

Cody's arm jerked up. "That way!"

Ben straightened. I shaded my eyes and squinted across Rankin, the road at the edge of the neighborhood.

Ben squinted against the glare. "You mean the leftover piece of woods?"

When I moved here, there was a whole lot of woods on the other side of Rankin; then the county bulldozed most of the trees so they could mine sand. For some reason a few fenced-in acres were still there, all woodsy and viny and surrounded by a split-rail fence.

Cody pushed the hat back to see where the hat had led them. "Oh. Never mind. Those woods are off-limits. Dad said." Then he told the hat he was sorry because he couldn't follow its instructions. He scuffed a sneaker in the roadside dust. "Guess we should go home now."

Looking at Cass and Big, I could tell that, like me, they were ready to turn back, but Ben crossed his arms and stared at the sandy pit the city kept digging deeper. "Remember when we used to build forts all over those woods?"

Cass smiled. "And remember that old car we used to hang out in?"

Big and I didn't remember any of that stuff—we were both too new to the neighborhood—but Ben and Cass were little together. They built forts, ran under the sprinkler in their diapers. His little-kid handprint is right next to hers on the cement in front of her house.

"And this is all that's left—the last wilderness." Ben peered into the forbidden woods. "Why does everything I want to do have a fence around it?"

"I take it you're talking figuratively, not literally," Big said.

I remembered the English class when Mr. Butler explained the difference—I thought Big mostly slept through Butler's class.

"Or," he said, "are you actually saying you've always wanted to go into that particular weed patch?"

"Guess I've never thought about it," Ben admitted. "But it's not like we have anything better to do. So what do you say?" Thumbs shoved into the pockets of his jeans, Ben nodded toward the woods across the glaring-hot tar road. "The fence is falling over anyway. See how it's leaning?"

"No," I said, "but I *do* see plenty of poison ivy climbing up that tree, and loads of sticker vines."

Cody's head bobbed. "Leaves of three, don't touch me!"

But when Ben gets an idea, his ears turn off. "If that land is abandoned—and I say it is—that means it's public domain. And *that* means we can take a look. What could looking hurt, anyhow?"

"But Ben," Cody whined.

Ben held up his hands. "Hey, just following the command of the almighty hat!" He loped across the street and climbed over a section of the fence that looked weathered but still stood pretty straight. "Come on!" Sitting on the top rail, he waved us across Rankin. Cass went first, then Big. What the heck. I jogged across too.

Cody stood all by himself on the other side of the street. "You guys! It's private property. Dad says!"

Straddling the fence, Big slapped his neck. "If it is, I just killed one of the security guards."

"I don't see any No Trespassing signs." Ben opened his arms. "Do you?"

Cody turned in place, scanning the fence from one end to the other, searching for signs. "Well, maybe just one look would be okay." He trotted across the street, holding the hat in both hands.

We all sat up on the top rail of the fence, our legs dangling above a patch of sticker vines.

Ben pointed out a strip that cut back into the woods where the brambles grew lower. "Looks like there used to be a road here, or maybe a driveway. It's gotta go somewhere."

"Doesn't mean *we* have to," I said. Sitting on that fence, it was hot and still. Hot and still and buggy.

Ben jumped down, took a few steps, and looked back. "Ya comin'?"

The rest of us just stared at him—he was the only one in jeans. Big was the first to cave. "Okay, okay!" He lumbered down off the fence. "If this isn't enough fun, we could try poking out our eyeballs with sticks."

Ben looked at Big's pink legs, then at me and Cass and Cody, still perched on the fence. "Never mind. You guys wait here. I'm goin' in." Ben let out a whoop. Lifting his feet high, he bounded over brambles and cut around saplings, zigzagging his way through the deep weeds until he disappeared. I expected Cass to leap down and run after him, but she stayed put, swinging her legs and holding her hair up off her neck.

"Reprieve!" Big climbed back up.

When we couldn't hear Ben anymore, we listened to the buzz of mosquitoes.

For a second, Big hummed that same mosquito note. "Ah yes," he said. "Summer's greatest hit."

Cass

Jemmie swung her legs back and forth, her flip-flops dangling. "Girl," she said, staring at my bit-up legs, "if you sit on this fence much longer, you'll have as many bites as you have freckles."

True. And I have a lot of freckles.

I was scratching my knee when we heard Ben yell, "Over here!"

Justin sat up straight. "Sounds like he found something."

Jemmie and me looked down at our bare legs, then out at the mess of prickers and vines we'd have to wade through.

"Can we ignore him?" Jemmie asked, but Justin was already on the ground.

"The torture begins," he said, taking a step into the weeds.

"This better be good." Jemmie slid down off the fence.

I climbed down too. Everybody follows Ben. Anytime he's a part of something, everybody else wants to be a part of it too.

"Come on!" Ben shouted. "Get over here!"

"He sounds pretty far away," said Justin, lifting a foot high to take another step. "These woods must be bigger than they look, like the TARDIS in *Dr. Who*."

Jemmie and me traded looks, then stared at him.

"You know, the phone booth that's bigger on the inside than the outside?"

"Follow my voice!" Ben yelled.

Cody was still sitting on the top rail. His skinny white legs were bit up bad too. I went over and turned my back toward him. "Grab on." He wrapped his arms and legs around me and held the hat in one hand, dangling it over my shoulder. It tapped against my shirt with every step.

Justin picked up a big branch. "To lift vines and kill snakes," he said. "If necessary." He glanced at Jemmie to see if she was impressed, but she was standing on one foot, looking for a place to put the other foot down.

It wasn't *so* bad once we got going.

There were a few clear spots, and not all the weeds had thorns. Some had flowers. "Bend down," Cody ordered. When I did he picked one, then stuck it behind my ear.

We'd been walking for what Justin called eons when I heard running feet, then a *whoop*, and Ben loped out from behind a big magnolia. "You won't believe what I found!" He grabbed my elbow and pulled me and Cody around the tree. Jemmie and Justin followed.

"Wow!" Cody said. His breath was hot and damp on my cheek.

"Wow is right!" said Ben.

Nobody else said a thing. We didn't know what to say about an old building in the woods.

"Don't you see?" Ben gave us a look like he couldn't believe we didn't get it. "The place is abandoned."

"And...?" asked Justin.

Ben held out his arms, then let them slap down at his sides. "Do I have to spell everything out for you people? We have a place now."

"A place sealed up tight as tuna in a can," Justin pointed out. Some kind of wooden shutters, hinged at the top, had been lowered and were nailed to the window frames on the sides and the bottom.

"Wonder what this place was used for," Jemmie said. "It's kinda small to be a house."

"A garage, maybe?" Ben folded his arms and stared at the building. "Probably not. No bay door. A workshop? Who knows? Who cares? With a few tools it won't be hard to get in. This place'll make a great hangout."

Cody slid off my back. "And Detective Dobbs led the way!"

"Way to go, Dobbs!" Ben high-fived his brother.

"Wait!" I said. "We're going to break in? Somebody *owns* this place."

Detective Dobbs looked back and forth between me and Ben.

"Come on, Cass," said Ben. "Lighten up."

"Yeah, lighten up," his little brother echoed, but he didn't sound as sure.

Justin scratched an ear. "Has anyone but me noticed it's really hot and buggy here?"

"Bet it's cooler inside." Ben shoved a hand in his pocket, dug out his pocketknife, and studied the closed knife. "Wish this thing had a screwdriver." He slid it back in his pocket.

Jemmie began walking heel to toe around the building, counting the size out in flip-flops. "Sixty-eight feet—*my* feet, that is." She glanced up. "I wonder where the house is."

We all looked around.

No house, but there was a big open spot where the sun came through and lit up the brambles extra-good.

Whistling, Ben disappeared around the side of the building.

I crossed my arms hard. "I don't think we should do this." But no one was listening.

"Needs work," Ben called. "But it looks good and sturdy." I heard a scraping sound. Ben was dragging down a broken branch that hung over the edge of the roof.

He came back around front and squinted up at a dead tree that stood real close to one wall. A silvery branch hung right over the roof. "That limb's gotta go!"

Justin jerked the padlock on the door. "Anybody got a piece of wire? Maybe I can pick this."

"You know how to pick a lock?" I asked, hoping he didn't.

"I saw someone do it on TV. It didn't look hard."

Cody set the hat down on the gray cement step by the door, pressed his palms together, and bowed. "Thank you, O Magical Detective Dobbs Hat."

Swept along by Ben, everyone was getting excited. Everyone but me.

If we got caught breaking in, Ben would be grounded, but he was used to that. Jemmie would get what Nana Grace called a "come-to-Jesus talking-to." Justin's parents wouldn't even care.

Nobody but me had a father who would kill them if they got caught breaking into a place that wasn't theirs.

Besides, breaking in was wrong. Somebody owned the building and the stuff inside it. I hoped it'd be too hard to get in and they'd get hot and tired and give up.

"Voilà!" Justin held up a rusty nail he'd found in the dirt by the steps and stuck it in the lock.

"Hey, Ben!" Jemmie called. "This shutter's kind of loose."

Maybe I should head home. I turned and saw Cody wandering away, kicking through the leaves. When he reached the open spot where the sunlight fell through the trees he yelled, "Ouch!" Hopping on one foot, he grabbed the toe of his sneaker.

"You okay, Cody?" By the time I trotted over to him he was scraping the ground with his sneaker, raking the damp leaves away.

"What're you...?" he mumbled. He grinned when he saw me. "Hey, Cass! Take a look. I found a sidewalk."

"A sidewalk?" I dragged a sneaker along the edge of a long concrete slab, walking away from Cody, step after step until it ended.

Then I realized, all I'd done was reach a corner. When I dragged a foot along that edge, it went on and on too. "Cody, I think you found the house."

He blinked at me. "What house? There isn't any house!"

"Not anymore, but I think this is a foundation." I cleared another patch of the slab with my sneaker. Instead of being light gray, this concrete was dark, like pencil lead.

Cody held up a charred piece of wood. "What's this?"

I dropped to my heels in a squat, suddenly scared. "Cody? This house burned down."

"It did?" he squeaked.

Walking toward me, he kicked a blackened shoe out from under the leaves and stopped dead. "What if there's a burned-up foot in that?" he breathed. He inched away from the shoe, then sat down cross-legged and stared at it.

"Ben?" I headed back over to the garage. "Ben, can I talk to you?"

He gave the shutter one more hard pull, then let go. "What about?"

"Cody and me found the house—what's left of it, anyway. There's a foundation and charred wood all around. The place burned down to the ground. I think we should get out of here."

"Okay." He shrugged a shoulder up to wipe sweat off his face.

"Really?" I didn't expect him to give in so easy.

Cupping his hands around his mouth, he announced, "Okay, people, we're heading out to eat and get some tools."

"No, Ben. Cody's scared." I put a hand on his arm. "I don't think we should come back."

Ben twisted away from me, grabbed the magic hat off the step, and strode over to his brother. "What's up, Detective Dobbs?"

Cody looked small, sitting with his arms around his knees.

"You…feel…anything, Ben?" he whispered, still staring at the shoe.

"Yeah." Ben lifted the front of his T-shirt and wiped his face. "I feel hot and hungry. Let's go home, grab us some lunch, pick up a few tools, and see what's inside this building you and the hat found." He dropped the hat on Cody's head.

Cody sat under the hat, breathing slow, his striped T-shirt sticking to his skin. "The hat says it made a mistake. This isn't where it wanted you to go. It says it will take you to the *real* place tomorrow."

"We'll help you find the real place," I said, jumping right in. I knew there was no real place, but I for sure didn't like this one.

Ben nodded toward the building. "Cody, tell the hat we like this place fine."

Cody pushed the hat back, but it fell over his eyes again. "Let's ask Dad if it's okay."

"*I'm* in charge of you this summer, remember? And I'm telling you it's okay. This place was abandoned years ago." Ben lifted the hat, then set it back on Cody's head like it was a crown or something. "Thanks to you, Detective Dobbs, summer is looking up! Now, come on!" He hauled Cody to his feet. "We got things to do."

I pointed back at the burned shoe. "Ben? What about that?"

"Yeah, what about that?" Cody echoed.

Ben slung his arm around Cody's shoulders, turned him away from the shoe, and started walking. "See, this is what happened. The shoe was in some closet when the fire started."

"Oh no!" Cody tried to turn back, but I saw Ben's fingers tighten on his brother's shoulders.

"Don't worry. The guy who owned the shoe ran out in his bare feet, and he was fine. In fact, everyone was fine."

"Except the shoe," Cody said.

Ben stopped and turned Cody toward him, his hands on his

brother's shoulders. "You *do* know shoes are just things, right, and that it's no big deal if they burn up?"

How would Ben know for sure that the guy who owned the shoe got out? But Cody was nodding—and I was too.

It's easy to believe a thing when you want to. And we both wanted to believe Ben.

CODY

All Cody could see of his brother from where he sat on the hood of Dad's latest project car was the butt of his jeans and the soles of his sneakers. Kneeling on the garage floor, Ben was digging around in one of Dad's tool drawers.

"Screwdriver." Ben's arm jetted out and slapped the tool into Justin's open hand.

"Screwdriver," Justin repeated.

While Ben clanged around some more, Cody hung the hat on the hood ornament, a pointy silver star that stuck up between his knees.

Out went the arm again. "Pliers."

"Pliers." Justin grabbed the next tool.

"Duct tape."

"Duct tape." Justin shoved the roll of tape over his chunky wrist. "Why duct tape?"

"You can fix anything with duct tape," said Ben.

Cody sniffed. The garage smelled like motor oil—a Dad smell. "Ben, are you allowed to borrow Dad's tools?"

More clanging. "Crowbar."

"Crowbar."

Cody bounced his heels against the grille of the car.

Ben stood, boosted himself onto Dad's workbench, and grabbed a can of WD-40 off a high shelf. Dad had so much junk, he had shelves up to the ceiling. "Catch, Jus."

The can hit the floor and rolled under the car.

Looking down between his own feet, Cody watched Justin belly-crawl under the car.

"I hope this stuff isn't like soda," Justin mumbled.

Ben jumped down and pointed at Cody. "Bust a move, Detective Dobbs! Get into some long pants, sneakers, and socks. Go!"

"But I'm hungry," Cody whined.

"Don't give me that. You just ate lunch."

Cody sighed, then picked up the hat. He swung his leg to one side of the throwing-star hood ornament and slid off the car.

He thought about the burned shoe as he walked through the garage door and into the house, wondering again if there might be burned-up toes inside it. He felt kind of barfy, like the time he ate a whole bag of Cheetos watching a baseball game with G-dad.

Halfway up the stairs, he stopped and settled the hat on his head. "Something really bad happened there, didn't it?" Cody whispered.

He didn't hear an answer, but it seemed like the weather inside the hat suddenly turned damp and cold.

"Thought so." He wanted to go back to not knowing stuff he knew now. Back to being plain old Cody. He took the hat off again and turned around on the step. The closet door was just across the room. He could put the hat back on the shelf.

But plain old Cody without the hat was like a tail on a dog, always wagging behind. Detective Dobbs led the way.

He sighed, put the hat back on, and trudged up to his room.

Jemmie

t isn't legal," Cass said as we walked toward Ben's house. "We're breaking in!"

"Like anyone cares," I shot back. "Nobody's been there for years." Both of us had changed into long pants and shirts with the sleeves rolled up. I'd ditched the flip-flops and put on sneakers—my toes were still itchy from this morning.

"Seriously, Jemmie. Don't you think it's wrong?"

"We'll probably take one look at the junk inside and close it up again. You know Ben won't let it rest till he sees what's in there." Even though Nana Grace says 'curiosity killed the cat,' I wanted to see too.

My friend's face lit up. She waved both hands. "Hi, Ben!"

Ben and his brother were sitting on the steps of Big's porch. Ben's school pack leaned against his leg. A metal bar stuck out the top. Cody's detective hat sat in his lap.

"Justin's putting on long pants," Cody whispered as we trotted up.

"I wouldn't mind if yesterday's T-shirt went too," I said, plopping down next to Cody.

Cass perched on the porch rail. Watching Ben, she swung her legs, flirting. I noticed she didn't say a word to *him* about not liking the break-in.

"Awful quiet in there," Ben whispered, looking back at Big's front door.

"His parents can't fight *all* the time," Cass whispered back.

"Why're we whispering?" I whispered.

"So they won't hear us." Cody leaned in closer and cupped his hand to my ear. "His parents are dangerous."

The door flew open and Big stumbled out, along with a whiff of bacon and a few notes of someone singing off-key.

"Everything okay in there?" Ben asked.

"Dad's on a cooking rampage."

"Oh, yeah." Ben slung a pack strap over his shoulder. "The apron and singing thing."

"Pretty much." Justin thumped down the steps.

I jumped off the top step to the ground. "What're you two talking about, aprons and singing?"

Big rolled his eyes toward Ben. "You had to go and bring that up?"

"Well?" I nudged his shoulder with my fingertips—he *was* wearing a clean shirt.

He stared for a second at the spot where my fingers had been. "Yeah, well, when Dad's trying to get back on Mom's good side, he turns into the psycho chef and puts on her "Kiss the Cook" apron. He clangs pots and pans around, sings in French—crap like that."

"That doesn't sound so bad," I said.

"Actually, it's pretty scary. After cooking and singing comes the next fight. Things are either crazy-good or crazy-bad at my house. We don't do normal."

I pointed at his clean shirt. "You play golf?"

"Golf?" Big glanced down and read the letters, upside down. "'A REAL SWIIIIIINGER!' Double-crap. It's my dad's." His ears turned pink. "We have laundry issues."

He needed a Nana Grace at his house, and not just for laundry. She'd straighten out his parents too.

Embarrassed, Big said, "Let's do this thing," and broke into a jog. Fine by the rest of us. The pack slapped Ben's back as we jogged down the street.

But in a few seconds Big slowed to a walk. "On second thought, what's the rush? We have all summer." I could hear him breathing through his mouth. Big doesn't have much run in him.

We climbed over the fence and cut into the woods.

At first we couldn't even find the garage. We went to where we thought it was, but it wasn't.

Big rested his hands on his thighs, panting. "All right, who moved it? Cass?"

My best friend crossed her eyes at him.

We circled back and tried again. A couple of times Ben looked at Cody like he was going to ask him to put the hat on, only that would be like saying he believed in magic hats.

After a while, Cody disappeared under the hat, but it didn't help.

"Bet we went too far," I said. It was awfully hot to be chasing around after a building nobody could find, not even the hat.

Just then Cody whooped. "Hey! There it is! Straight ahead, guys."

Dark and solid between the trees, I don't know how we missed it. It was suddenly there, like someone had just plopped it down.

"Way to go, Cody!" Ben tried to give Cody a high five, but ended up high-fiving the hat Cody held up.

"Way to go, hat!" Cody whooped, sticking out his skinny chest—since he'd found the hat, Cody was feeling pretty good about himself.

Ben turned back to the building, his knuckles on his hips. "It's bigger than I remembered."

"True," Big agreed. "Usually things seem bigger when you think about them, but not this time."

Cody danced from foot to foot, proud about finding the place with the help of the hat. "I bet there's a lot of cool stuff in there!"

Cass hugged herself. "But none of it is ours."

"True," said Cody, swinging the other way. "None of it."

Ben dug through the pack and came up with a screwdriver. He rammed it into one of the screws that held the metal hasp to the door. Big watched—like Ben needed an audience to use a screwdriver. I wasn't about to stand around and watch Big watch Ben. I grabbed the crowbar out of Ben's pack and worked the flat end under the edge of a shutter. "Come on, Cass. Help me."

Four hands would've fit fine on the crowbar, but Cass folded her legs and sat on the ground. Cody copied her. She twisted the end of her ponytail around her hand. "I think this is called breaking and entering."

While I yanked on the crowbar, Ben messed with the first screw, but he couldn't budge it. "Rusted in tight." He held out his hand and Big slapped a can of WD-40 into it. Ben sprayed the screws and handed the can back.

I clutched the crowbar in my sweaty hands and pulled hard, but nothing happened. "Put the can down and get over here, Big, I need your weight."

He looked stunned—sheesh, I didn't mean it like *that*.

"One megaton, coming up." He put the WD-40 on the step.

I slid my hands down the warm metal bar. "Grab ahold."

He gripped the free end in both hands.

"On three," I said. "One...two...three." We leaned back and the nails made a little squeak, but they didn't pull free. "Again, Big! We're getting it!" This time we threw ourselves back hard, but the crowbar popped loose and flipped out of our hands.

Big went down, flat on his back. I crash-landed on top of him, my cheek mashed against his neck, feeling his pulse. I took a sharp breath. Up close, Big smelled sweet, like cherry Kool-Aid.

"Sorry," he gasped. "Sorry. I didn't know the power of my own weight! Sorry if I'm sweating on you! Sorry!"

"It's okay." I pushed up on my arms. I'd never been this close to him—or any guy—unless I was stealing a ball.

I dusted myself off like it was no big deal. "Let's try again, but this time, hold back a little."

We tugged at the crowbar again, but standing next to Big was different now. I kept wondering about the cherry Kool-Aid smell and feeling like we were still touching. "How are you doing with those screws, Ben?" I asked.

Ben thumbed the last screw down into his pocket. The lock was still locked, but the piece of metal that attached it to the door frame swung loose. "We're good to go." But Ben didn't open the door. Now that it was time to see what was inside, he was stretching it out.

"You want to bet the big prize turns out to be a push mower and a couple of dented garbage cans?" said Big.

Ben grabbed the doorknob, then hesitated. "Cody? You wanna do the honors? You led us to this place."

Cody walked over to the door slowly. He gripped the knob, let the hat drop over his eyes, and froze.

"What're you waiting for?" Ben asked. "Permission from the hat?"

I nudged his shoulder. "Do it!" I said. Even in pants and long sleeves I was getting bitten up. I lowered my voice. *This is the hat speaking.*

Cody stood, hand on the doorknob. "That's not how the hat talks, Jemmie."

While we waited for the hat to give Cody the go-ahead, Ben fished two flashlights out of his pack and handed one to Big.

"All right, Cody. What's the word from the hat?" Ben asked.

Cass

Cody stood with his hand on the knob, looking really little under that big hat. Ben tapped the toe of his sneaker, impatient like always. "Don't rush him," I said.

Cody was thinking about saying no, I could tell. No, because his parents wouldn't like us breaking in, and no, because of the sad, burned-up shoe.

"Cody? We're waiting." The hand on Cody's shoulder squeezed.

"Don't give me a yes-squeeze, Ben!" Cody complained. "The hat is thinking...and the hat says..." Cody tugged gently on the knob, but nothing happened. "Maybe...no."

Ben slapped a hand over his brother's. "You just have to yank it harder."

The hinges let out a long *skreak* as the door swung open, but we couldn't see much. It was awful dark in there.

"Smells like attic," said the voice from under the hat. "Attic mixed with Dad's garage, library books, and wet dog."

Jemmie sneezed.

Justin aimed his flashlight and clicked it on.

Standing behind the others I couldn't see much, but the beam of light looked cloudy, like the air was full of dust.

"Happy Halloween, people," Justin said.

A scared whisper came from under the hat. "Ghosts?" Then louder, "Skeletons?"

Jemmie bumped him as she bent forward to look inside, and Cody yelped. But no one was paying attention to him—they were all straining to see what was behind the door. I leaned in close and whispered, "Take off the hat, Cody, it's okay."

"You sure?" He pushed the hat back and blinked.

Ben ran his flashlight beam up to the ceiling, then whistled between his teeth. "Talk about abandoned." Spiderwebs clung to the rafters. "Come on, guys. Let's see what we've got." Jemmie and Justin followed him inside.

I hung back with Cody. Standing outside the door, I couldn't see much. All the shutters were still nailed tight. "What're you doing?" I asked as Jemmie dragged a finger across the top of a bookcase.

"Writing my name in the dust. J...E...M—" She squinted at something, then forgot about writing the rest. "Hey, cool!"

She crossed in front of the open door, then disappeared. When she came back, she had something in her hand. As soon as she moved behind the other side of the door, something flew across the dark space. *Thwack.* "Bull's-eye!" she yelled.

It didn't seem right throwing darts, or writing in the dust—but it did seem as if no one had been there in a long time.

A dart in one hand, Jemmie walked up to the open door and leaned out. "Come on, you guys," she said. "Take a look around. This place is so abandoned, nobody even remembers it."

Cody stuck his head in the door. "For really?"

I stuck my head in too. It was pretty dark in there, dark and full of stuff, like it had been used as a storage shed or maybe a workshop.

Justin swung a broom, tearing down a spiderweb. The spider dropped to the floor.

"No!" Cody yelled, but it was too late.

Justin lifted his shoe and checked out the sole. "That was gross."

"No killing spiders!" said Cody.

Ben grinned. "Yeah, forget killing spiders. That's rule number one for our new clubhouse, right, Cody?" Now that we were in, Ben could afford to be nice to his brother.

"Good rule." Justin dragged his shoe across the floor, wiping off dead spider. "It's too messy."

"And be respectful to the stuff in here," I blurted out. "Because it isn't ours."

Ben pointed his flashlight up, skipping the circle of light across the ceiling. "The place seems tight and dry."

Justin swept down another web. He looked at the spider wobbling on the broom, then at Cody and me. He walked to the door and tried to shake the spider off the bristles. When it hung on, he leaned out the door and banged the broom against the side of the building. "Go free, wild creature!"

"That's a *house* spider!" Cody said.

One more bang, and the spider fell off the broom like a fluff of dog fur. It landed in the dirt near my foot. "Not anymore," Justin said.

Hands on his knees, Cody leaned over the spider. "You sprained his legs, Justin!"

But Justin was already sweeping down the next web.

Ben came back out whistling and picked up the crowbar. I put a hand on his arm. "Ben?"

He shrugged my hand off. "Would you just relax?" Crowbar swinging, he went around the corner of the building. I tucked my hair behind my ears and started to follow him.

"Hey, Cass." I felt Cody tug the leg of my jeans. "The spider's limping!"

I knelt down with him and we watched. "Don't they kind of always walk like that?"

Behind the building a nail squealed, then another one. The squeal came again and again.

As I looked through the door, a bar of light appeared. It got wider as Ben lifted the shutter. It disappeared for a second, then came back as Ben propped the window cover open with a branch. On the other side of the dusty screen Ben was just a gray shadow until he put his face up close. "Cody, Cass, go on in."

Cody looked up from the limping spider. "You wanna, Cass?"

"Might as well." I heard another nail squeal as Ben attacked the next window.

Cody grabbed my hand and jumped through the door, pulling me along.

Before I could look at anything, Cody was showing me the shovel he was going to "borrow" so he could dig up the dinosaur bones in his backyard faster.

"This isn't our stuff, remember?"

He bumped the hat in his hand against his thigh. "I forgot." He leaned the shovel up in the corner again, right where he'd found it.

Jemmie shoved a dart into his empty hand.

"Hey, bop-a-loo-bop," he whispered. The dart missed the board and bounced off the wall.

"Try it with the hat on," Justin suggested.

Cody looked at the hat in his hand, but didn't put it on. "I don't *always* want the hat telling me what to do." He glanced toward the window Ben was prying open. "I get bossed around enough."

Hinges creaked and light poured in a second window. Ben shaded his eyes on the other side of the screen. "Hey, are those games on that shelf over there?"

I walked over and read the names on the sides of the dusty old boxes. "Monopoly, Parcheesi, Candy Land. You like board games, Cody. Want to play one now?"

"No thanks. Spiders or something are living in them—I'll bet Monopoly is someone's home."

I stepped back and bumped into something that bumped me back.

"Birdcage," said Cody when he saw me jump. "No bird, though. That's good. It would be a skeleton by now."

The cage swung gently from its hook. The bars were knit together with dust and spiderwebs. Everything in that room was so furry with dust, Jemmie could've written her name anywhere.

Cody fanned his face with the hat. "Say, are you guys hot?"

We were all hot, but nobody said so.

Ben pried open another window, and light fell on a small table I hadn't seen before. I took a step toward it. "Oh, look! A sewing machine!"

"A sewing machine from back in the day," said Jemmie. "Like the one Betsy Ross sewed the flag on."

It did look almost that old. Hanging on the back of the chair was a pattern piece pinned to a double layer of fabric. Like the patterns in the old box Mama had in her closet, it had solid lines for seams and dotted lines for darts. "Looks like someone was making a dress." Careful not to lean against it, I sat, pulled out the edge of my T-shirt, and took a swipe at the sewing machine table. Beautiful gold leaves and flowers appeared.

Mama used to make most of our clothes on her portable sewing machine, until my older sister, Lou Anne, complained that everything looked too homemade. But Mama's machine, with its plastic case the color of a Band-Aid, wasn't pretty like this one.

I lifted the piece of cloth that dangled over the edge of the table. The seam was sewn only halfway; the needle was still through it. It looked like a sleeve for the cut-out dress that hung on the chair back.

Jemmie stuck her head under the sewing machine table. "You

68

think this treadle makes it go?" She rocked it with her hand. The needle lifted out of the fabric with a little *click* and bobbed down again. "This is great! It doesn't even need electricity!"

I picked up the end of the unfinished sleeve and turned it inside out. Although the outside of the sleeve was dusty, the good side of the purple satin with tiny pink roses was like new.

"I wonder why this dress was never finished." As I smoothed a finger across the fabric of some other girl's dress, I shivered—then glanced over my shoulder, but it was just us and the spiders. Cody lifted his head and took a sniff. "You guys smell anything?"

"Yeah," Justin said. "Dust and spiders."

"No, I mean like smoke," Cody said.

He was thinking about the house that had burned down—and that bothered me too—but looking at all the spiders and dust, it seemed as if Ben was right. The garage and everything in it had been forgotten a long, long time ago. And if that was true, maybe what we were doing wasn't so bad.

The tissue pattern piece crinkled as I hugged the cut-out dress against myself. When it was sewn, this would be a dress for going to a dance. I glanced at Ben, who was up on a chair, dragging a box off a shelf.

Daddy finally agreed to let me go to the last dance in middle school, but he made Mama chaperone. A high school dance would be different…and Ben would have a lot of girls to choose from besides me. But what if I was wearing a satin dress with pink roses?

I looked at the thin paper pattern pinned to the cloth and jumped, like I'd stuck myself with one of the pins. "Jemmie, see the size? That's *my* size."

She stared at me wide-eyed. "It's like it was meant for you."

ben

Sweat trickled down my back—it was hot all right, even working in the shade. Lucky thing this was the last window I had to uncover.

Between the heat and the bugs, it was going to be hard to keep everyone excited about this place. Jus didn't like to sweat in front of Jemmie. And Jemmie'd have more fun doing something with a ball in her hands. Even with the sewing machine, Cass probably still thought that busting into this place was wrong, and I could tell Cody was kind of spooked.

I was the only one who thought this was a great idea—make that the *only* idea. We needed something to get us through what Cass kept calling "our last summer."

I gave one more pull on the crowbar and the nails along the third side of the shutter jerked free. When I lifted it, light flooded the back of the garage. I peered down through the dusty screen at something big pushed up against the wall. It was covered with a cloth, but the shape was unmistakable. "Hey, Jus, over here."

Justin turned and stared, then he got this big, goofy smile.

I jogged around the outside of the garage, grinning too. If the piano under that cloth still played, I wouldn't have to convince Justin to come out here.

As I walked inside, he jerked the fabric back and said, "Merry Christmas, Justin Riggs!"

He dropped the cloth on the floor, then slowly lifted the lid that covered the keys. It hit the piano with a hollow boom as he folded it back. I would've tried it out right away, but he stood there and shoved his hands in his pockets.

"Bet it's *way* out of tune," said Jemmie.

"Maybe not too bad," I said, walking over to Jus. The piano keys were yellow like dog teeth, except the ones that were the dingy gray of old glue. Some of the ivories had fallen off.

"It's probably *way* bad," Jus admitted. He ran a hand along the keys too lightly to make them play. "But it's a piano!"

Jemmie put her hands on her hips. "Guess this means you don't need to play *my* piano anymore."

"Sure I do!" Justin said fast. "But this one is more…mine." He put a hand on top of the piano. "I claim this piano in the name of Justin Riggs, aka Big." He glanced over his shoulder at Jemmie. "To be played when the piano belonging to Jemmie Lewis is otherwise occupied."

"Shouldn't you see if it still plays before you go claiming it?" Jemmie asked.

Justin dragged a finger through the dust on the piano bench, shrugged, and then sat. He pushed one key down and held it. The note quivered.

"Sounds pretty good!" I said.

"One note?" said Jemmie. "Play something, Big."

Justin began to play some piano-book thing. The notes were a little plinky, but inside that old garage they didn't sound half bad.

"No C-sharp," Justin mumbled. He stopped playing whatever he was playing and struck each key with a finger. "No G." He winced when the next key clunked. So, it wasn't perfect.

"But it's a piano, right?" I said.

"Yeah." Jus ran his hand lightly over the keys again and smiled. "Yeah, it is." And I knew my best friend was in.

A sudden motion caught my eye—my little brother jumping back as he let out a girly squeal. "Snake!"

"Where?" Cass lifted her feet.

Cody pointed at a dark coil that looped out from behind a chest of drawers.

I pulled it out. "It's just a hose."

"Oh," he said. "I knew that."

Down on one knee, I spotted the toolbox shoved into a corner. "Well, look at this." I dragged it out and opened the lid. "Great. Now I won't have to borrow Dad's tools."

"Cool!" Cody said. "You gotta show him."

The wrench I'd picked up clattered back into the box. This was the part I was afraid of. Cody the Mouth blowing everything. "Listen up." I stood, spun a chair on one leg so it faced me, and straddled it. I gripped the chair back and looked at each one of them, hard. Cody the longest and hardest. "We tell no one about this place."

"How about Leroy?" Jemmie asked.

"No." Justin glanced at her over his shoulder, his fingers still on the piano keys. "Think about it." Then he did a little Leroy rap. "We got the goods, found 'em in the woods, we broke right in, now gimme some skin."

Jemmie frowned. "We *have* to tell him. He's part of us."

Jus stared at his fingers on the keys—I know he was trying to cut out the competition, but he was right about not telling Leroy. The fewer the people who knew, the less likely it was someone would leak. Tell Leroy, and Jahmal would know—and pretty soon everyone would know. Including Dad.

"He doesn't need this place," Justin mumbled. Then louder, "Leroy's busy turning pro. And Anna's in Brazil seeing the rain forest, and Clay's in Indiana seeing…whatever's in Indiana." *Plunk.* He struck a sad chord. "We're the left-outs…" *Plunk.* Another sad chord. "The losers…" *Plunk.* "Until Cody and the hat found this place, nothing was going to happen to us but a long"—*plunk*—"hot"—*plunk*—"summer. We deserve this place."

I held up a finger. "So, rule number one."

"Not killing spiders is rule number one!" Cody whined.

"Two, then."

"Respect for stuff," Cass said, fanning herself with an old *LIFE* magazine.

"Okay, rule number three—but this is the important one. We tell no one about this place."

Cody looked anxious. "Except Mom and Dad?"

I put a hand on his shoulder. "We tell nobody, especially not parents."

Cody opened his mouth to object, but I made my voice deep, like Dad's. "Little bro, don't even *think* about this place around them."

He clenched his fists. "Why can't we tell them? We're not going to hurt anything."

I blew out—this was complicated. "*We* know being in here is okay. But they're parents. It's their job to worry about stuff that isn't going to happen. They think we're helpless."

"And irresponsible," Cody added.

"I'm responsible. Responsible enough to be in charge of you this summer, so if I say something is okay, it is. And I say being here is okay. Are you in, Cody?" I tipped the chair up on two legs and leaned toward him. "Or are you going to wreck it for everyone?"

He raked his sneaker across the floor, watching the lace drag. "The hat said not to open the door!"

"The hat was just messing with you. It brought us here in the first place. In or out, Cody?"

"I guess…in."

"Good man!" I held up a hand and we slapped high five—his slap was kind of wimpy, but I'd work on his attitude. He'd be okay.

Jemmie bounced her heels against the side of the flowered armchair she'd fallen into. "We should give this place a name."

Cody suggested Spider House. I could've gone along with that. But Justin played that fast run he calls an arpeggio. "How about Nowhere?" he asked. "That way when someone asks where we're going, we won't be lying."

Cody took a couple of steps toward the center of the room and waved his arms. "Hey, guys, look at me! I'm in the middle of Nowhere."

"Good one!" said Justin. He began banging out something that sounded like a march.

"What are you playing?" Jemmie asked.

"The Nowhere anthem."

"I hope it's easier to sing than the national one," she said.

I hung my arms over the chair back and relaxed a little. At least for the moment, everybody was on board. And, at least for the moment, summer was showing some potential.

Cody was marching in time to our anthem when he suddenly stopped dead.

I figured he'd spotted another hose-snake, but he was staring at a dusty sleeping bag, crumpled in a corner with something that looked like the corner of a magazine sticking out the top.

His knees hit the floor, and he grabbed the magazine and pulled it out. "Guys, look! A Spiderman comic!" But there wasn't just one. Someone had stashed a whole collection of comics in that bag. This was better than I could have hoped for. There was something here for everyone.

Cody opened a comic and let out a yelp. "B-ben!" He stabbed at something on the first page.

"Wha-what?" I walked over. "What're you stuttering about?"

His chewed-down fingernail took another jab at something written in blue ink. "You see what that says, Ben?"

I saw—and a tingle walked up my spine.

Written inside the cover was a name I knew real well.

Paul Cody Floyd

COdY

ody didn't want to be Nowhere anymore. He didn't get why his missing uncle's name was on the comic, and it scared him. "Can we go now?"

Ben said, "Later," then called him a baby when he said he wanted to go *right now.*

Cass took one last look at the cut-out dress on the back of the chair, then stood up and stretched her arms over her head. "I'll walk Cody home and feed him—as long as you get there by one, Ben." She had to watch her little sister in the afternoon while her big sister went to beauty class.

"What do you feel like for lunch?" she asked Cody as they tromped through the woods.

With the hat swinging at his side, he stared up into the trees. "Something…creamy."

They looked in his refrigerator and the pantry. The creamiest thing they could find was a jar of peanut butter. She made him a sandwich and carried it to the table.

Cody pulled out a chair. "Why do you think Uncle Paul's name was in that comic?"

"Bet your uncle knew the people who owned the garage." While he chewed, she told him what she remembered about his uncle from when he'd lived with his family. "He was real skinny, with long hair. My father called him 'the dirty hippie.'"

"My dad has a ponytail," Cody reminded Cass.

Cass made a face, like her father didn't like Dad's ponytail either, but then she added, "Your father has a regular job. Your uncle just hung around." While Cody ate his sandwich, she told him about how his uncle gave them piggyback rides, and how he used to shoot hoops in the street and plunk on an old guitar. "Most of the time Uncle Paul was fun, but sometimes, not so much. Sometimes he wouldn't even get out of bed."

"Not for all day?" Staying in bed all day sounded boring to Cody.

But Cass nodded. "Yes, for all day."

At 12:57 she said, "Gotta go," even though Ben wasn't there yet. "Just stay out of trouble till he gets here." Cody could tell she was mad at Ben.

☺☺

He was lying on the couch when the door slammed and Ben fell into the living room, panting.

Cody lifted his head and looked at his brother over the hat on his chest. "Hi." He put his head down again and folded his hands.

Ben collapsed onto the couch, breathing hard. "You look like… you're ready for…your own funeral."

"Just staying out of trouble. I promised Cass. You weren't here and she had to get home so Lou Anne wouldn't kill her."

Ben stared at the ceiling. "That means Cass is going to kill *me*."

"You *are* pretty late."

"I lost track of the time. After you left I found some cool stuff, even an old ladder, so I climbed up on the roof."

Cody propped up on his elbows. "Find anything more of Uncle Paul's?"

Ben shook his head. "Nope."

"How do *you* think his comics got in that sleeping bag, huh?"

Ben said pretty much the same as Cass. "He must've known the people who lived in the house."

Cody sat all the way up. "The house that burned down!"

"Yeah, but the two aren't connected. Kids have friends. Kids trade comic books. Houses burn down." Ben shoved his legs out straight. "End of story."

Cody looked down at the hat. *End* of story? He didn't even know the beginning. "Cass made me a creamy peanut butter sandwich. I'll fix you one."

"Don't want a sandwich." Ben rested his neck on the sofa back and stared at the ceiling.

"No sandwich, coming up." Cody got the jar of peanut butter and stuck a spoon in it. He held the jar out for Ben, then pulled it back to his chest. "But you have to eat at the table." Mom's rule.

"Nah. It's not like peanut butter drips." Ben snagged the jar and dug out a spoonful. "Maybe I *am* kind of hungry." He stuffed the spoon in his mouth.

When Cody parked cross-legged on the couch and turned toward his brother, Ben lifted his eyebrows.

"Oops," Cody said. "Forgot." Mom didn't like sneakers on the couch either.

Ben shrugged. "Mom's not here. It's okay with me if you go rogue."

Still, Cody hung his legs over the side. "Cass told me about Uncle Paul, how he used to ride kids around on his back."

Ben laughed. "Cass was way too tall for piggyback. Her feet practically dragged! Uncle Paul was fun."

"Cass said not always. She said sometimes he just stayed in bed.

Was he real tired?"

Ben dug out another spoonful of peanut butter. "Yeah. Tired of Dad yelling at him."

"Dad yelled at his own brother?"

"Sure did."

Cody couldn't believe it. He leaned toward Ben. "What else do you remember?"

"Not much."

"Come on, Ben. Tell me!"

Ben stopped with the spoon halfway to his mouth. "I *do* remember he called you 'Squirt Gun.'"

"Why?"

"You were just learning to use the toilet. Get it?"

Cody felt his face get hot. "Was Uncle Paul like Dad?"

Ben snorted. "No."

"How were they different?"

Ben put his feet up on the coffee table—Dad had a rule about that, but Ben smacked his heels down, *thump, thump.* "Pretty much every way."

"Name seven." Cody got so close he could smell peanut butter on his brother's breath when Ben blew out a sigh. "Okay, okay! Just tell me one."

"All right. One. Dad's a rule-follower, like you. Uncle Paul isn't."

"I'm not *that* big a rule-follower." Cody slid down on his butt bone and tried to smack his feet up on the coffee table too. "Like right now? I'm not following the rules. It's just that my legs are too short!" He swung them against the couch until he looked down and saw he was leaving a mark. "How else were they different?" He hoped Ben would forget he was only going to name one difference.

"Uncle Paul smoked. Clean-living Dad never did. Uncle Paul was trying to quit, but that didn't get any sympathy from Dad. Rain or cold, Dad made him smoke outside." Ben spooned up a giant glob, but he didn't put it in his mouth. "Sometimes he'd climb into one of the project cars, sit in the driver's seat like he was going somewhere. I'd sit in there with him."

"And breathe secondhand smoke!"

Ben cut his eyes Cody's way. "Yup, it was crazy-dangerous. Probably took years off my life."

"About how many?" Cody whispered.

"I don't know…could be…any minute now…" He grabbed his throat, rolled his eyes back, and fell against the couch, gagging.

"Be-en!" Cody whapped his brother's arm.

"Sissy slap!"

"I was being nice. I can slap harder!" He inched a little closer, thought about slapping harder, but didn't. "What else do you remember?"

"Nothing much. One day, I went to school and when I got home—*poof*—he was gone."

"Oh my gosh!"

"Don't get all excited. I didn't mean *poof,* like magic."

"Of *course* not, but I know about when Uncle Paul left," Cody whispered, leaning in. "Dad told me."

"Really?" Now Ben leaned toward him. "What'd he say?"

"This?" Cody held the hat out to his brother. "Uncle Paul bought it for a job interview. Dad set the whole thing up. Uncle Paul got the job too, but he only went a couple days. Then he just… quit."

"So?" Ben shrugged. "Dad decided what was good for his brother and pushed to make it happen, then blew up when Uncle Paul didn't go along? Big deal. He gave the job a try and he didn't like it."

"You don't understand. Dad got him a job. A *real* job. For money! And Uncle Paul quit. And then? After he quit? He just disappeared!"

Cody watched the corner of his brother's mouth twist down. "I wonder," he said. "Did he 'disappear' or did Dad kick him out?"

"Dad wouldn't do that!"

"I bet he did." He flicked the postcard in the hatband with one finger. "I'm surprised he even sent a postcard after Dad kicked him out."

The Space Needle was facing Ben, but Cody could see the squirrelly handwriting on the back, especially the message on the corner. He thought about Ben sitting in the passenger seat while Uncle Paul smoked. "You said he called me Squirt Gun. What'd he call you? Shotgun?"

Ben turned away.

"Was it Shotgun?" Cody asked.

jemmie

Ben had taken off for home when I yelled up to the roof that it was after one and that Cass had to get home. I'd head home soon too, but for now it was just me and Big in the Nowhere garage.

Me, Big, and "Clair de Lune"—his assigned piece for the week. He played it over and over, until he was wearing it, and me, out. "You sound ready for your lesson."

"Yup." Still staring at the keys, he smiled. "Real ready."

I was never "real ready" for my lesson, even when I could play every note. When I played for Mr. Butler, even *I* could tell something was missing. "Feel the music," he'd say. "Slow down and *feel* it!" I could slow down, but all I felt was the urge to play that draggy old music faster.

Listening to Big, I got what Mr. Butler meant. Big played "Clair de Lune" different each time. Sometimes slow, sometimes fast, but always "with feeling."

After a while, the tune began to wander.

"What's the matter, you forget how it goes?"

"Nah. I just got tired of going there." His head sank lower and his bangs hung over his face as the notes crescendoed—that means they got louder—with feeling.

Without a piano, Big was like Nowhere before we broke in. No way in, and who knew what junk might be inside?

With the piano, it was like he'd opened the door, just a little. I could stick my head inside, shine a flashlight in—not that he'd notice me looking around.

When Big played, he wasn't showing off for me, or anyone. He was playing for himself like no one else was in the room.

I grabbed a musty old book off a shelf and flopped into the flowery armchair again. I opened the cover of the book and sneezed. "Clair de Lune" had shifted into something like a storm on the ocean—all low notes. He'd stop, then play the storm again.

I wondered, could I even get his attention? I waved—he should be able to see me from the side without even turning his head. I waved again but the music had taken him somewhere else. Fine. I'd let the words in the open book take me somewhere else too.

England.

That's where the story was set.

I read a page and a half and yawned. England sure was boring.

I looked up at Big, pouring the music out, and jittered the leg that hung over the side of the chair. I looked some more, trying to see Big as, you know, a guy. He's sort of chunky, like he still has his baby fat, and he's the kind of white that turns pink in the sun, or if he gets embarrassed.

I scratched my itchy knee. Big kept pouring out his stormy melody. This place was hot and the Nowhere piano was out of tune. It was time to go.

I hung the open book on the arm of the chair and walked over to the piano.

Duh, duh, duh… I hit the first three notes of "Heart and Soul." He joined in with the chords, not missing a beat.

Finger still on the key, I parked my butt and shoved him with my hip so he'd give up a few inches of bench.

When I reached the end of the melody, I started over. *Duh, duh, duh...* By then our four hands were flying. His two were as white as Wonder Bread and chubby—but fast! Wish he had the same touch with a basketball.

Back when we first started playing this tune together, I was better than him—but he'd left me behind. Now he could play things I'd never learn. I was a pro at "Heart and Soul," though, so I went on and on with the stupid *duh-duh-duh* melody.

As his notes danced around mine, I glanced at him. At the piano, Big looked different—serious, and almost good-looking. Almost.

I picked up the pace, playing faster. Big gave me a look like *You gotta do better than that*, and suddenly he was playing really, really fast—so I played really, really fast too.

This kind of piano playing I got. We were in a "Heart and Soul" race and I wasn't about to let him beat me.

I could feel the sweat on my forehead, but I went even faster. He pushed back, making *me* speed up until I went, *duh, duh, duh* on the wrong key. I threw my hands in the air. "I give up!"

He looked surprised. "So, I win?"

"What do you mean, win? Playing the piano isn't a sport!"

"The way you play, it is."

"Yeah, kind of." I dragged a finger down the white keys.

His hands dropped into his lap. "Good. Because it's the only sport I've got."

"Yeah, you are the 'Heart and Soul' king." My face got even hotter. "I mean, the 'Heart and Soul' *piano* king."

"Right."

I jumped up from the bench. "Race ya back to the neighborhood."

"To even the score?" he asked as I put a hand on the door. "One to one?"

I stopped. "What are you talking about?"

"One for the music man, one for she-who-runs-with-wolves."

"Only if I win the race."

"When," he said. "*When* you win. Me beating you in a footrace would be like you beating me at 'Heart and Soul.' It's not going to happen."

"Who says I could never beat you at 'Heart and Soul'?" I stood with my feet wide apart. "I'll be back for a rematch—and maybe I'll win next time. At least I'll try. You give up before you even start."

"Yeah, well." He lowered the lid over the keys, the same old Big who would rather drop a basketball than take a shot. "It saves time."

"You want to really save time? Run!" I turned and dashed out the door, knowing what would happen next. Big would dawdle along after me, like I'd never challenged him to a race. Sometime next week we'd sight him back in the neighborhood.

I heard the thud of footsteps behind me and glanced over my shoulder. Big was running! "Ow!" he moaned. I didn't look back again. Whatever the "Ow!" was about would be an excuse to give up. Now that he was injured, it would take him *two* weeks to limp home.

The "Ow!" was followed by more thudding, then an "Ouch!" I slowed down a little. Why totally embarrass him? At least he was trying.

A hand touched my arm.

"Could you pick it up a little?" he panted.

Justin

Can't breathe. Can't think. My heart's about to blow. I'm dying. Seriously. Dying.

Why did I tell her to pick it up?

She glares at me over her shoulder, and then she does, she picks it up.

And then I do too.

I never run except PE laps, where I almost always come in dead last—but now I'm flooring it! Bet Jemmie's surprised. But not as surprised as me.

She's ahead, but I charge through a bunch of stickers like it's a shortcut, trying to catch up.

Great. Now I'm bleeding. I haven't actually looked because I'd have to slow down, but I must be, because the skin on my arms and legs burns like fire-ant bites and I feel trickling. Unless it's sweat. Why do I always have to sweat in front of Jemmie?

Maybe I should stop running and watch her disappear between the trees.

Maybe I should just die and get it over with.

Maybe there's a hole in the middle of my chest—it sure feels like it. Pretty soon my heart's going to fall out. Jemmie will probably laugh.

The weirdest part is not the fact that I'm dying—it's the fact that I'm keeping up.

"Pick it up or get out of the way," I wheeze. Am I nuts?

Her head whips around. She looks back at me over her shoulder—and her dark eyes with the little yellow flecks in them get wide like she doesn't believe what she's seeing. "Don't worry. I'll get out of your way! No more Mr. Nice Girl!"

I should've known she was holding back—it's just that I'd never seen her do it before. Mr. Nice Girl is not Jemmie's style.

She takes off, running flat out—and I do too. We roll over the fence at about the same time. She steps into the road just a little ahead of me. We stop, both of us gasping. "You...win."

"Just barely," she admits. "You...really ran."

I groan. "But why?" I drop to my knees in the middle of the road and slump to the asphalt, then roll onto my back and fling my arms and legs out. "That was painful...horrible. My lungs...are inside out." I look over at her. "You do this for fun?"

"You play piano for fun." She sits down on the curb.

I suck the air in, but there isn't enough oxygen in it. It's like diet air. "I am never...ever...moving from this spot."

"Don't you have a piano lesson today?"

"Not till three." When I glance over again, she's got the heels of her sneakers up against the curb and her skinny arms around her knees, watching a sweatball who can't catch his breath.

I am lying in the middle of the street like a roadkill possum, but staggering to my feet would be too embarrassing and probably not possible at this time. I close my eyes.

"Don't you go falling asleep!" she scolds.

How do I get out of this one? Not sure, so I shrug my shoulders like I'm settling in. "Actually? This is pretty comfortable. You should try it."

"No way." I hear the tap of a sneaker. "You think I'm crazy?"

"How do you know it's crazy till you've tried it?" I ask, keeping my eyes closed.

No answer. Maybe she's silently sneaking away.

But the next thing I hear is a loud huff, and when I look she's sprawled out beside me on the road not three feet away.

This is seriously weird.

We stare into the oak that hangs over the road. "This road stinks," she says.

The fumes from the warm tar *are* pretty strong, but not bad. "I kind of like the smell." I shrug my shoulders again. "The road feels good against your back, doesn't it?"

Out of the corner of my eye, I see her shrug too. "It's okay."

On the sunny side of the street we would fry, but here in the shade the road feels almost cool on my sweaty skin. I lift my arms, finally strong enough to do it, and check out my wounds. "My arms look like the time I tried to give Gizmo a bath."

"You got scratched up pretty good." She makes it sound like a compliment.

When I let my arms fall, my knuckles brush hers. She whips her hand away and pretends she needs to tug her shirt down. Bet she wishes she'd sprawled farther away.

She folds her hands on her stomach. "Wonder what would happen if someone came peeling around the corner?"

I turn my head and look at her. "Splat?"

What would Ben think if he saw me and Jemmie Lewis lying on our backs on Rankin?

I hear her sneakers scrape as she bends her knees. "Big? How long are we gonna lie here smelling the road?"

"I dunno. I'm comfortable."

"Me too," she admits. "Guess we'd better put up a sign."

"What kind of sign?"

"Speed Bump."

I laugh. "Hey, that was funny."

"You think funny is your department?" She sits up fast. "I can be funny!" She jumps to her feet and goes.

"Okay!" I yell, listening to her sneakers slap the pavement. "I'll give you a head start."

tuesday
(seven minus five)

COdY

Floaty and half-asleep, Cody heard Mom singing downstairs. "'Blacks and bays…dapples and grays…all the pretty little horses.'"

"Toast?" Dad's voice.

"'Way down yonder…in the meadow…'"

A basketball hit the floor. "Not in the house, Ben." Mom sang the words like they were part of "Pretty Horses."

Coffee smell sneaked up the stairs.

Cody opened his eyes and pushed up on his elbows. Everything in his room looked as gray as the hat that hung on his bedpost—everything except the postcard. A skinny finger of light poking between the curtains hit it like a spotlight.

Remembering his uncle's name scrawled in that comic book, Cody crawled to the end of the bed and stared at the Space Needle. This time, instead of a covered platter of fried chicken, he saw a spaceship.

Maybe Uncle Paul was abducted!

But he couldn't say that to his family. They laughed when he'd asked if eating too much broccoli could turn him into broccoli—even though he *did* look sort of green.

They laughed when he asked them if a tidal wave might hit

Tallahassee, and if it did, would there be sharks in it? "Cody and his wild imagination," they said.

But was it wild to wonder about an uncle no one had heard from in years?

He felt a sudden shiver, then remembered what he'd heard Nana Grace say: "A shiver means someone's walking on your grave." Even though Cody was pretty sure he didn't have one, the word "grave" made him shiver again.

He stood on the bed and grabbed his uncle's fedora. "Come on, hat."

He jumped off the bed, then hopped down the stairs on one foot—lucky left. As his foot hit the floor at the bottom, he remembered what day it was. Seven minus five.

He stopped in the kitchen door. "Hey, how old will Uncle Paul be on our birthday?"

No one answered. Ben was watching the numbers on the microwave go down and Dad was pouring a cup of coffee. Mom, just humming now, looked up from the newspaper. "No hats at the table." As Cody sat in his chair, she took the hat off, kissed the top of his head, and then rubbed her mouth.

"Tickle-lips?" he asked.

"Tickle-lips."

Cody's summer haircut had bristles.

"How old will Uncle Paul be?" he repeated.

"Twenty-nine." Dad opened a cupboard. "How about some breakfast, Sport? Let me guess." He snapped his fingers. "Cereal?"

"What else?" Dad knew he *always* had cereal.

"How can you stand eating the same stuff every day?" Ben sucked up a snake of spaghetti, spraying his lips with tomato sauce. "You may not have noticed, little bro, but your life is pretty boring."

"Guess what we found yesterday?" Cody blurted.

Ben's eyebrows shot up.

"What?" Dad glanced at Ben. When he turned away to hand Cody the Cheerios box, Ben gave Cody the laser look.

"Oh, nothing." He shook cereal into his bowl carefully, so the Os would land one at a time. *Ping...ping...ping...*

"Ben?" Dad wasn't smiling. "Watching your brother is your summer job. No disasters, remember? We're counting on you, and you're getting paid, so be responsible."

Cody glanced back and forth between his brother and Dad. Ben stared right back at Dad like he had nothing to hide.

Nothing but a whole building he'd had to pry open!

"We're not getting in trouble," Ben said.

Dad turned. "Cody?"

Cody pushed a Cheerio under the milk with his spoon and waited for it pop back up. It didn't. "We're not getting in trouble." He added a silent *yet.*

⊙⊙

Mom and Dad hurried out the front door, ready for work, but Dad stuck his head back in. "To repeat: No disasters, Ben. Are we clear on this?"

"Crystal." As the door closed, Ben swung around. "Cody?"

Oh man, he was going to get it now!

"We gotta talk." Ben squeezed the back of Cody's neck and propelled him toward the living room, then let go and plopped down on the sofa.

Cody flumped into Dad's recliner, keeping his distance. "You lied to Dad."

"No, I didn't!" Ben frowned. "Maybe I didn't exactly tell the truth, but you weren't supposed to say anything about what we

94

found! We all agreed that was rule number one."

"Number three!"

"Yeah, yeah, spiders and stuff."

Cody rubbed a finger back and forth on the arm of the recliner. "I think they should know about it."

Ben crossed his legs. His sneaker lace jiggled as his foot bobbed up and down. "This is a need-to-know situation. If there's a *reason* why they should know, we'll tell them. I promise." He uncrossed his legs, put both feet flat on the floor, and leaned toward Cody, resting his forearms on his thighs. "Here's the thing. We've lived in this one place our whole lives. And nothing ever happens here."

"I like it here."

"It's okay when you're little, but wait a while and you'll feel like"—Ben stared at the ceiling light for a second—"like a car with its engine revving real fast but there's no way to get out of park. You know what I'm talking about?"

"I guess." Ben and Dad compared everything to cars.

"So, here we are, stuck in park, probably for the whole summer, and then you make this great discovery. Do I think Dad would put the place off-limits if he knew about it? I sure do. But will anything bad happen if we don't tell him and just keep going there? No. Why would it? Dad's a worrier. He always expects the worst."

Cody popped his thumbnail back and forth over a seam on the chair arm. "Ben? That place feels creepy."

"You imagine stuff, Cody. Remember the time you had a bad feeling about leaving your socks under your bed 'cause you thought they'd grow and turn into monsters overnight?"

"I was little then!"

"Or when you thought your toys came to life when you were out of your room?"

"I didn't really!" Cody shrugged. "Not for long, anyway!"

"You're big now. Almost seven, old enough to think for yourself.

So, think about this. Take away Nowhere and all we have ahead of us is a long, hot summer." He held up his hands, then slapped the couch on either side of him. "What do you say? Are you going to tell like a baby, even though you promised not to?"

"I *said* I wouldn't tell!"

"Great! Perfect! Just don't forget." Ben grinned. "We'll seal the deal with a little Moose Tracks." He headed for the kitchen.

Armed with spoons, they each dug out one big bite of ice cream. This was another thing Cody wasn't so sure about. Ever since the last day of school, Ben had waited until after Mom and Dad left for work, then he'd broken out the ice cream so they could each take a bite.

Ben tossed his spoon in the sink. "Think of it this way," he said. "I'm in charge of you when Mom and Dad are at work. If I say a thing is okay—like hanging out at Nowhere—it's okay."

"And like stealing ice cream?"

"Who's stealing ice cream?" Ben put the carton back in the freezer in the exact spot where he'd found it. "This is *our* house, *our* freezer. Besides, Mom and Dad hit the Moose Tracks every night after we go to bed. As long as we don't take too much, they'll never notice."

Cody wondered, Did Mom and Dad's not noticing make it okay?

Justin

I wake up to the hum of Gizmo's purr motor as our old cat dozes on my chest. I lace my hands behind my head and smile at the ceiling.

Not a bad day yesterday.

Good, actually.

Better keep that at "not bad." Why tempt the joy-crushing forces of the universe?

But it isn't like the universe can make yesterday un-happen. For instance, my piano lesson with Butler. At the beginning of the year Butler was nothing but the massive English teacher who drummed rhythms on his desk with a couple of pencils. Then I discovered that, like me, he had music playing in his head 24–7. With him teaching me, the music in my head is finally getting out.

My biggest Butler worry now is not how to stay awake in his English class, but how to get to his house for piano lessons. My drivers are unreliable.

Yesterday Dad dropped me off, then headed to the driving range. I worried that he'd forget to pick me up—but I forgot about Dad as I played "Clair de Lune." I tried to stick with the piece the way Debussy wrote it, and not mess with the man's notes.

When I finished, Butler wore this little smile. "Now play it again—the way *you* would have written it."

So I launched. When the last note died out, Butler folded his hands over a gut that makes mine look like a six-pack. "Mr. Riggs. As an English student, your performance is quite mediocre, but as a piano student, you show great promise. I have never had a student learn so quickly or display such creativity. You are, quite simply, the best I've ever worked with."

My face heated up. I'm used to being called mediocre, so that was no biggie. But I've never been called the best—at anything.

Butler reached over and played a quick flourish on the low notes, a bit of the melody I had just played. Then he let his hands fall to his knees. "You are very fortunate to find out at such an early age what you are."

I'd been called a lot of things, none of them exactly complimentary. "What am I?" I asked, staring at the keys.

"A musician!"

"A musician," I whisper now. I scruff the cat behind the ears. "How about that, Giz? Butler says I'm a musician." I think about telling Mom. Dad wouldn't care, but Mom might.

I raise my head and listen to downstairs. Silence, then the microwave beeps. Somebody's up. After that beep, more silence.

Silence is okay, if only one of them is up. And if only one of them is up, I hope it's Mom.

I lift the Giz off my chest and set him on the pillow, then dress for Nowhere in long pants, socks, and sneakers. I roll up the long sleeves of my shirt—even in the AC I'm sweating—then I grab the open bag of bedside marshmallows and stuff them in a cargo pocket. I walk past my brother's empty room—Duane is in the Army—slip past my parents' closed door, and go downstairs.

They're both in the kitchen, wearing their matching blue bathrobes.

Mom isn't talking.

Dad isn't talking.

I've seen this before. The frozen argument.

Mom drops a piece of bread in the toaster and slams the lever down. Although they aren't talking, they can turn anything—even making toast—into part of the argument.

Best course of action? Act like nothing is wrong and get out fast. "Good morning, you guys."

Dad grunts. I just see the top of his shiny bald head above the *Democrat*.

"How was your lesson?" asks Mom.

It's probably not the time to tell her I'm the best, so I shrug. "It was okay."

"I still don't get the lessons." Dad lowers the paper and gives me one of his just-between-us-guys smiles. "We don't even own a piano."

"True," I say. "But we could get one."

Dad laughs like I'm joking, then turns to Mom, who stirs her coffee loudly, clanking her spoon against the cup. "Does this piano thing seem crazy to anyone but me?" he asks.

When she doesn't even look at him, he turns to me and holds up his hands like he just doesn't get it. "The lessons cost money, and as soon as you discover girls you'll forget all about playing the piano. It's kind of sissy anyway."

I stare at my sneakers. Way to go, universe. Set me up with a good day, then knock me down. "Mr. Butler says I have a lot of talent," I mutter.

Dad shrugs. He sells restaurant equipment up and down the East Coast. What does he care about musical talent?

But Mom drops her spoon on the counter. "Are you dismissing your son's talent?"

He puts on a crooked smile, like, *Can't you take a joke?* "No. I'm just glad to hear he has one."

If Dad could pick a talent for me, it wouldn't be music. He

keeps telling me I'm built for football. Excuse me, but I like music a lot better than knocking people down.

Dad turns around in his chair and stares at the smoking toaster. His eyebrows, the only hair on his head, lift. "Kathy, I believe your toast is ready."

Forget breakfast. I'm out of here.

Before the door even closes behind me, I'm nailed by the morning heat.

So much for my "great day." In case you haven't noticed, the universe has a mean streak. I won't be surprised if the hideout Cody and the Wonder Hat found has been crushed by the dead limb Ben wants to cut down.

When I see the roof between the trees, I let out my breath. The limb is still waiting to fall. Sooner or later it will, though, or else Cody will leak and tell his parents, making the place off-limits. But until then I have a place to go besides Ben's house. A place with a piano.

I pull the door open and walk quietly across the room. I sit down at the piano, rest my palms on the cool wooden lid, and let out a long, slow breath.

I lift the lid and strike middle C, holding the key down until the note dies out. Then I begin to play "Clair de Lune," my way. It's hard to ignore the old piano's sour notes, or the G, C-sharp, and D that don't play at all. I wish I had a Steinway like Butler's.

I walk my fingers up and down the scales.

It worries me when my dad talks like he might not go on paying for lessons, but he can't take away what Butler said. That part of my good day was real.

I'm kind of scared to think about the other good part of my good day. I tell the universe, Look, it probably didn't actually happen, so what is there to take away?

But the facts are undeniable. Jemmie and I *did* lie down on the road together and talk. And for a while she acted (or sort of acted) as if she (kind of) liked me.

Needing a little sugar to help me think, I pull the sack of marshmallows out of my cargo pocket and pop two in my mouth, a pink and a yellow.

Okay, "liked" is probably too strong a word. At best, Jemmie tolerates me.

But yesterday?

Yesterday she tolerated me for a really long time.

CODY

The push broom thumped Cody's shoulder as he marched through the woods behind Ben. "Do I look like a soldier?"

Ben stopped and turned. He cocked his head.

"Well?" Cody marched in place. "Do I?"

"You would." Ben grinned. "If soldiers were four feet tall, wore detective hats, and shot people with brooms."

Cody pointed at the two paint scrapers sticking out of his brother's jeans pockets. "You look like the Wild West."

Ben snatched the paint scrapers out. "Stick 'em up!"

But Cody swung the broom off his shoulder extra fast. "*Bam!* Too bad. You're dead."

"The shame!" Ben grabbed his chest and staggered. "Killed by a janitor!" He shoved the scraper handles back in his pockets. "C'mon."

"Hey, hear that?" Cody pointed at the garage, barely visible through the trees.

The notes of the Nowhere anthem drifted toward them. Cody marched ahead of Ben, leading the way to the garage.

When they got there, Ben grabbed Cody's broom and put a foot on a rung of the rickety ladder leaned against the roof. "Go on inside." He scrambled up the wobbly ladder.

Cody tipped his head back. "Can you see our house?"

"No. Just trees."

"Can I climb up too?"

Ben looked down on him. "You heard Dad, no disasters. Besides, I'm not up here to have fun. I'm gonna sweep the leaves off, then see what kind of shape the shingles are in. Go in and say hey to Justin."

"I want to go on the roof too!" Cody kicked at a pile of damp leaves and bumped something hard. "Wonder what's under there," he mumbled.

He found a stick and dug, uncovering a cloudy semicircle sticking up from the mud. He scraped away leaves and dirt until he could pull it out. A drinking glass. It was old and dirty, but not broken. He held it up. "Hey, look!" he yelled, but the only answer was the sound of sweeping. He stared at the glass. How long had it been lying there waiting?

He scooted a beetle out of the glass and wiped it off with his T-shirt. The music got loud when he shoved the door open. Justin's shoulders twitched but he didn't turn around.

Cody slid onto the piano bench next to him.

"Hey, Jem—" Justin turned Cody's way and blinked. "Oh. Hi, Cody." He nodded toward the open bag on top of the piano. "Want a marshmallow?"

"Look at this!" Cody shoved the drinking glass into Justin's face. "I found it buried in the leaves."

Justin leaned back for a look. "A dirty glass. Cool."

Cody set the glass on top of the piano carefully, right exactly in the center, then stuck a muddy hand in the bag and grabbed a pink marshmallow.

From overhead came a scraping sound. A dark blob fell past the window, followed by a *whoosh-splat*. Justin flinched. "What was that?"

"Ben's sweeping leaves off the roof." Cody hit the highest note on the piano. *Plink.* "Think I'll go out to look for more stuff."

Justin held up the murky drinking glass. "You really think you can top this?"

When Cody walked out the door, Ben yelled down at him, "Where are you headed?" He rested the broom against his shoulder. "We are *not* going home."

"I know."

Ben wiped his forehead with the shoulder of his T-shirt. "You can't even get into the house. I have the key around my neck."

"I'm only going to here." Cody stepped up on the foundation of the burned house.

"Just stay where I can see you." Ben shoved another pile of leaves off the roof.

Cody looked down. There was that shoe. It was still lying there with its tongue hanging out. Cody took a raspy breath. He knelt down and checked the shoe for dead toes. Empty. He let his breath out.

He turned in a circle, then stopped. He hadn't noticed before, but a weird mound sat right behind the foundation.

Like everything else, it was covered with leaves and branches, but something was underneath it, making the bump.

He found another stick and poked it into the pile. The leaves were wet and heavy. It took two hands to circle the stick around, making a hole. Suddenly, something went *dink*, like the dull sound of the broken doorbell at his house.

Hands on his knees, he leaned forward and peered in. He saw something shiny. Another drinking glass? He reached for it, but the hat slid over his face. "Hey, you gotta let me see." He kicked the leaves off a corner of the concrete slab, then scraped the surface clean with the side of his shoe and set the hat down.

He reached into the hole, farther this time, and touched something smooth and cool.

The lid on the blue bottle he pulled out was rusted tight. He grabbed it with the edge of his shirt, twisted it off, held the bottle up to his nose, and gagged. "Gross!" Whatever was inside smelled like the stuff G-dad rubbed on his knee joints when they ached and pained.

He tried to screw the lid back on, but it wouldn't go. He emptied some thick brown goop into the leaves and put the bottle next to the hat.

He found a stapler and a clock—the kind with hands. A fishing reel with the line all melted and a ceramic dog dish, charred black, but with letters dented into one side. He rubbed dirt off with his thumb and read, "Sparky."

He kept digging and finding. Before long the hat had plenty to look at.

When he stood up from the pile, wet leaves stuck to his arms. He balanced the clock on top of the bottle. Maybe he could stack everything up and make a… He couldn't think of the right word for what he was going to make.

He put on the hat and closed his eyes, and the word he was looking for fuzzed into his brain. "Thank you." He took the hat off again and set it down.

A split-finger whistle from up on the roof made him jump. "What're you doing, Detective Dobbs?" Ben had finished sweeping and was sitting on the roof watching him, sneakers dangling.

"Building a momunent!" he yelled back.

"That's mon-u-ment. A monument to what?"

Cody looked at his ring of discoveries. His eyes settled on the dog dish. "Sparky!"

"Who the heck is Sparky?" Ben yelled back.

Cody picked up the dish. "Sparky the dog!" When he set the dish down, his hands were all sooty. Forgetting Ben, he squatted and whispered to the dish, "You were in the house when it burned down, weren't you?. Was Sparky in there too?" Cody wondered if the family had called for the dog to come when they ran out. Or was Sparky like the shoe, left behind to burn to death? He glanced around. Would he find Sparky's bones under the leaves?

A sudden shadow loomed over him.

"Heart attack!" Cody yelled, grabbing the middle of his shirt.

"We've already been over this," Ben said, looking down at him. "You're too young to have a heart attack." He put a knee down on the slab. "Seriously, why are you stacking all this stuff up?"

"I already said. Building a momunent."

"Mon-u-ment."

"That's what I said." Cody nudged the bowl toward his brother. "You think the dog died in the fire?"

"No. Dogs are smart. Bet he went out the dog door."

"What if they didn't *have* a dog door?"

Ben kicked at the leaves and a doll's head rolled out. Half of the plastic face was melted, and through the hole Cody could see the wires that came out of the backs of the doll's eyes. Cody bit his lips, but he managed a weak laugh.

"It's just an old doll head." Ben picked it up and hurled it off into the trees like he was pitching a softball. "Say, what's that?" He pointed at a white loop poking up through the leaves.

Cody knew Ben was just trying to distract him, but he stuck a finger through the loop and fished up a coffee cup. "Look, Ben. It's Dad's!"

"No it's not."

"Yes it is!" It was the same as the heavy white china mug Dad used every morning. "Look! It even says 'Victor' on the bottom."

"I bet Victor made a million of those mugs."

Cody held the mug that was just like Dad's in both hands. "Maybe the dad who owned this mug died in the fire."

"Nobody died in the fire!"

"How do you know? Bet Dad would. He's lived around here his whole life."

"Yeah—that's why his whole life is so exciting."

"Come on, Ben!" Cody begged. "We gotta ask him."

"You *know* we can't ask Dad, but I'll find out about the people in the house, okay? The dog too."

"How? How will you find out?"

"Don't worry about it. I'll get you an answer."

ben

Jus tagged along with Cody and me when we went home for lunch. As soon as we were in the kitchen, Jus opened the refrigerator. "Got any soda?"

"Do we ever?" As long as we've been best friends, he should have known it was no use, but he still scanned the refrigerator shelves, cruising for something loaded with sugar.

"Would you get out of there? All we have is healthy junk."

"Yeah, but at least it's cool in here."

I shoved him aside and grabbed cheese and tomatoes.

"Want to wash up?" I asked my brother, like Cody ever wanted to wash up.

"No, I'm in a digging mood." He was looking out the window into the backyard.

"Go," I said. "I'll call you when lunch is ready." He was already black with soot from building his mom-u-nent. A little added dirt wouldn't make a difference; I'd hose him off before Mom and Dad got home. Besides, digging for dinosaurs would get him out of the house.

"Wonder where the girls were." Jus scrubbed his hands at the sink. "I thought they'd show up this morning."

"Me too." I hoped they weren't already tired of going to Nowhere. I tossed Jus a towel, then handed him a knife and a loaf of Mom's whole wheat bread and picked up the phone. Cass answered on the first ring. "Where were you?" I asked. She said she and Jemmie were watching Missy while Lou Anne gave practice haircuts at some nursing home.

"Missed you," she said.

I turned away from Jus. "Yeah, me too." When I looked back, he was grinning. I rubbed the back of my neck and turned away again. "Listen, you mind if I send Cody over for a while? He'd be glad to play with Missy."

She said okay and we hung up.

The bread knife hovered over the bread. "'Me too,' what?" Jus asked.

"Nothing," I mumbled. "And would you give me that?" I reached for the knife. The whole phone call he'd only cut one slice and it was fat at the bottom and skinny at the top.

"You don't like the way I cut bread?"

"No."

He dropped the knife on the counter. "All I need is practice. At my house the bread comes pre-sliced." He parked on a stool. "By the way, why're we getting rid of Cody?"

"There's something we have to do and Cody's got to be out of the way."

"Okay."

He didn't ask what. Jus is a go-along guy. Sometimes I wish he had an opinion, but his going along with me works most of the time. I cut five slices of bread. "Would you give a shout for the dinosaur hunter? I'll put everything on the table."

"Sure." He slid off his stool and stuck his head out the door. "Cody, if you're not having lunch with a T. rex, get in here!"

My dirtball brother came in breathless, clutching a bone he said belonged to an ancient baby dinosaur. Jus and I exchanged looks, but neither one of us let on that it was just a chicken leg bone. Cody was right about the ancient part, though. Nobody ever ate chicken in our house.

We built some powerful-thick sandwiches; Cody's was half mayo, the top slice of bread ready to skid. After we finished, he trotted off to Cass's with mayo on his chin and the ancient baby dinosaur bone in his pocket.

I booted up the computer in the den and got Google on the screen. Jus pulled a chair over and fell into it. "What're we looking for?"

"The fire. I told Cody I'd find out if anyone died." I typed in "house fires Tallahassee," and got 938,000 hits in .36 seconds.

"Video!" Breathing through his mouth, Jus reached across and clicked the mouse. Flames belched out windows. He leaned in toward the screen. "You think anyone's inside?"

"They wouldn't be shooting video if someone was inside."

"Never know. They might."

Jus doesn't have much faith in people.

The video ended with a frozen shot of smoke billowing. He mouse-clicked again. More flames. "We're looking for *our* fire," I reminded him.

"Oh, yeah. Only 937,998 more to check out—or we could limit our search. We're trying to find out if anyone died, right? Add 'fatalities.'"

I did and hit Enter. This time we got 132,000 hits in .44 seconds. Still hopeless, but I clicked through a few entries. Nothing about our fire. There were several articles on dead grandparents and babies in cribs, though—good thing I'd sent Cody to play with Missy.

"Check out this one." Jus stabbed the screen with a finger. "Seeing Eye Dog Ike Won't Leave Master, Dies in House Fire."

I fell back in Mom's desk chair. "This isn't getting us anywhere."

He pulled his chair closer. "Narrow it by date. It has to have been a while ago."

We decided to go back twenty years, coming forward one year at a time. Doing it that way there weren't so many hits and we moved faster.

We were scanning our fifth year when Justin said, "Bingo." Then he about toppled his chair. "Get a load of the date. It'll be exactly fifteen years next Saturday. Which is Cody's birthday."

I looked at him. "Also our Uncle Paul's birthday."

Then Jus read the headline. "'Three Perish in Southside House Fire.' The little dude isn't going to be happy about this."

I scrolled, he read. "'Killed in the late-night fire were Rowan Branson, his wife Fran, and their thirteen-year-old daughter, Lucy.' Holy crap!" He looked at me. "Guess we know why that dress Cass found on the sewing machine never got finished."

"And why it's Cass's size."

Jus read on. "'The only surviving member of the family was fifteen-year-old Coleman Branson, who was not in the house at the time. The cause of the fire is under investigation.'"

Jus sighed. "Well, that's it, then. Nowhere is history. Cody'll never go back."

"Sure he will." I clicked and the fire disappeared like it never happened. "He'll go back if we don't tell him."

"Wait. Weren't we checking this out because he asked?"

"Yeah, but I didn't think anyone had died. That's a huge deal. I'll bet my mom and dad knew them. Wonder why they never mentioned the fire... Maybe because it was so long ago."

"Didn't your dad say to stay out of that particular piece of woods?"

"Yeah, because it was fenced and had a couple of Private Property signs." I stared at the blank computer screen, beginning to wonder if that was the only reason. "Do we have to tell Cody about this?"

My friend's head bobbed. "Seems like it."

Fine time for Jus to go and have an opinion. "Why?" I asked.

"Okay, we won't—so much for truth, justice, and the American way." He shrugged. "Maybe you're right. After all, people die everywhere. Whether we're hanging out there or not, they'd still be dead."

"Indisputably." I thought for a second about Coleman, the sole survivor. He obviously hadn't come back in all these years, which meant the building really *was* abandoned.

"Do we have to lie to Cody?"

"No," I said. "We just won't mention it."

In about ten seconds we were both ready to return to our hideout. Any other day we might not have gone back—the afternoon was heating up—but it was almost like we expected it to look different now that we knew about the Bransons.

When we passed Justin's house, he detoured into the empty driveway. "Window of opportunity. Dad was in a good mood yesterday so he emptied Publix, and no one's home. Let's stock up."

He filled a couple of grocery bags with canned goods. Then he threw in a can opener and a handful of plastic forks and spoons.

"Your mom won't notice that all this junk is missing?" I asked.

"*Your* mom would. But my mom? The whole cooking thing takes her by surprise, like, 'What, suppertime again?' Trust me, she doesn't have a clue what's on her shelves."

The last thing he did before locking the door behind us was grab his brother's old sleeping bag out of the hall closet. I didn't ask why.

When we reached Nowhere, he moved the board games and wiped the empty shelf down with the kitchen towel he'd swiped. "We'll put the supplies here."

Beginning to unpack one of the grocery bags, I pulled out a little bottle. "Maraschino cherries?"

"They're primo on peanut butter sandwiches."

I squinted at the fine print on the label. "Sulfur dioxide, calcium chloride, and red dye number forty? This stuff would never get through the door at our house. Mind if I try one?"

"Help yourself."

The lid opened with a pop. I fished a cherry out by the stem, stuck it in my mouth, and groaned, "Red dye number forty is great!"

We finished off the jar.

"Wonder if we could paint this place?" I asked. Knowing no one would be coming back made me feel like Nowhere was really ours.

"I'll check our garage for paint. If there's any in there, Dad doesn't remember it."

"What *do* your folks remember?"

"The score." Jus wandered over to the piano, but instead of sitting down he picked up the drinking glass that sat on top of it. I figured he was thirsty, but he kind of flinched, then carried it over to me. "Cody found this." He forced it into my hand. "Does it feel weirdly cold to you?"

"Like some dead person was holding it?" I joked. "You're beginning to sound like my little brother."

൭൭

Cass and Jemmie were lounging in lawn chairs when we came to collect Cody.

Cass lit up when she saw me. "Hey, Ben!"

"Hey, Cass!" I called.

Jemmie and Jus purposely didn't look at each other, which I took as an encouraging sign.

I walked over to the sandbox where Cody and Missy were playing. The water-spotted hat sat in the grass next to the hose. Someone must've wet down the sand, and Cody too—he was almost clean. "Nice castle."

The chicken bone was sticking out of the top of one of the castle's sand towers.

Cody tamped down the wet sand in a yellow bucket with the back of a plastic shovel, then flipped the bucket over and pulled it off. "Ta-da! The last tower."

Missy made a fist and smashed it.

"Hey! I *told* you not to do that again!"

Giggling, Missy smashed another tower.

Cody threw a handful of sand.

Missy fired back and got him right in the face.

He grabbed a double fistful.

"Cool it! You're the big kid, Cody." I hauled him out by the armpits. "It's time to go anyway." Cass jumped out of her chair and picked up Missy, who was crying.

Cody twisted in my grip, then went limp. "You done?" I asked, setting him on his feet.

"I was tired of castles." Cody dropped the sand and wiped his palms on his T-shirt. He picked up the hat and started to put it on, then stopped. "What did you find out, Ben?"

"About what?" I felt my palms get sweaty.

He bounced on his toes. "About the people in the burned-down house?"

Justin gave me a look, like, *We are so busted.*

Why, this time, did short-attention-span-Cody have to remember what he asked me to do?

Cass quit brushing sand off Missy's legs. "Were they okay?"

I looked from Cass to Cody to Jemmie, then back to Cass. I hadn't planned to lie to everyone, just Cody, and only if necessary, but I could straighten the girls out later. "Uh, yeah. We found a newspaper report on the internet. The fire was fifteen years ago, ancient history."

"And…" said Cass.

I bunched my fists in my pockets. "And everybody got out fine."

"Really?" I could hear the relief in Cass's voice. "If everyone got out, I think it's okay for us to be there. If they wanted the stuff, they would have come back for it by now."

"Yippee!" Cody flung the hat up, then picked it up off the wet grass. "What about the dog?"

"The dog was fine," Jus said, giving me backup.

Cody stared at the hat in his hand, and for a second he looked much older than seven. "Are you sure?"

"Yup, Ike got out," I said, grabbing the name of the Seeing Eye dog from that other house fire story.

"But the name on the dish is Sparky," said Cody.

"Sparky was probably the dog before Ike," Jus said.

"Yeah. Ike was a golden retriever," I added, slapping on another lie like it was duct tape. "They all moved to Pittsburgh after the fire."

Cody yelled, "Great!" Cass gave me a hug.

Yup, duct tape can fix anything.

wednesday
(seven minus four)

Cass

Please, Cass…" My sister Lou Anne peered at me with one eye. The other one was hidden behind a curtain of blond hair. "Please-y, please? Would you watch Missy this morning? I have to study for a test!"

"If you have to study so bad, how come you had time to straighten and blow-dry your hair?"

"What do you think the test is on?" She picked up the hand mirror off the bed. "Does this hairdo look sexy?"

"What's so sexy about letting your hair hang in your face?" I grabbed my own hair back in its usual ponytail and twisted a rubber band around it. "You just want to get out of watching Missy."

"I do not! I'm practicing for my career!"

I rolled my eyes. Lou Anne had been practicing for her career her whole life—my sister has never worn her hair the same way two days in a row. "Come on, Lou, be fair! It's your job to watch Missy. I watched her yesterday."

She pooched out her lip. "Why won't you do it? You got nowhere to go!"

"You're right!" I snapped my fingers in her face. "And I'm going there now!" I ran down the stairs before she could make her eyes get all shiny, but turned back at the door and skidded to a stop. I yanked the string-and-stuff drawer open and got out the scissors—

Mama wouldn't miss them if I brought them home each night. The ones in the Nowhere sewing table drawer were rusty.

I trotted down our front steps, the scissors jouncing in my pocket. I felt better about breaking into Nowhere now that Ben had found out about the people who lived there, and I liked having a place that was sort of mine.

I've never had a room of my own. Lou Anne and I share—but the room feels like hers. I'd never paint a room of my own pink, and my room would never smell like hairspray.

As I cut across the yard going to Jemmie's, I caught a glimpse of the old rocker behind the rose of Sharon bush where I used to sit when I wanted to be by myself. I trotted over and put a hand on the arm. It wobbled. The joints had gotten loose sitting out in the weather. I hadn't gone to sit back there for a long time. I hadn't even thought about it or missed it.

Sometimes, I guess, things change without your even noticing.

I glanced at the knothole in the fence between my yard and Jemmie's. We used to talk to each other through that hole back when she first moved in and Daddy didn't want me talking with black people. But that was before he got to know the Lewises.

I sat in my old chair for just a second, my elbows on my knees. The chair felt rickety under my butt, and the sun was hot. Our last summer was ticking away, and I was wasting it!

I jumped up. Leaving the chair wobbling, I cut around the fence and sprinted up the Lewises' front steps. Jemmie's grandmother was dozing in her porch rocker with General Lee, their fourteen-pound tomcat, in her lap. Artie was pushing a toy truck around her feet.

"Morning, Nana Grace!" I called.

She startled awake, then smiled. "Oh, hello, Cass. This is some mighty drowsy weather. Go on in. Jemmie's upstairs reading."

I took the steps two at a time and fell into my friend's room. "Ya ready?"

Jemmie set down a magazine and stretched her arms over her head. "I guess."

Jogging in place, ready to take off, I patted the scissors in my pocket. "I'm going to finish that dress and you're going to help me figure out how to do it, right?"

When she nodded, I grabbed her arms and dragged her to her feet. "Come *on!*" And I shoved her toward the stairs.

"Where are you two going?" Nana Grace asked.

"Nowhere!" we said together.

We were jogging along, kind of easy, when Jemmie looked at me sideways. "Day before yesterday...?" She hesitated.

"Yeah?" Whatever it was, I knew she wanted to tell me.

"When Ben blazed out of Nowhere to take Cody off your hands, Big and I played 'Heart and Soul.'"

"The race?" I'd seen them do it, playing four-handed as fast as they could. "Bet he won."

"Now why do you automatically assume he won?"

Ever see someone run with their knuckles on their hips? Well, Jemmie can do it. It was her way of letting me know I was getting on her last nerve.

But then she grinned. "Okay, you're right. He won. He said the score was one to nothing, so I challenged him to race me back to the neighborhood."

We jogged across Rankin, me trying to imagine Justin lifting his feet. "And then he wussed out?"

"That's the weird part. He didn't." She vaulted the fence and cut into the woods.

I vaulted after her. "Justin ran?"

"Yup. And he almost kept up."

"Justin ran hard enough to keep up with *you?*" I stopped.

She stopped too. The skin on her neck glistened with sweat. "I said, almost."

"If he ran that hard, he must *really* like you."

She took off running again. "What is it with you and this boyfriend-girlfriend thing?" she called over her shoulder. "I just thought it was interesting, that's all." She leaped over a log and picked up speed.

I smiled as she flashed away between the trees. I knew something she didn't. She was beginning to like Justin.

And *I* liked the idea of my best friend and Ben's best friend liking each other.

jemmie

The roof of Nowhere came into sight. Was Big there? I didn't hear any plinky, out-of-tune piano. As we reached the clearing, a high-pitched voice called, "Hey!"

"Hey yourself!" I called back.

Cody was sitting cross-legged on the scorched foundation of the house, surrounded by burned-up stuff. "Look at this!" He held up an old bottle. "Wait." He wiped it with his T-shirt and held it up again.

Cass leaned over him, her hands on her thighs. "You're wrecking your clothes. Does Ben know you're playing with this stuff?"

"I'm not playing."

"Then what *are* you doing?" I asked. Looked to me like he was playing—and he was *definitely* wrecking his clothes.

Cody stood and brushed off his butt with his filthy hands. Ben would have some explaining to do when his mom tried to scrub those stains—his little brother for sure wasn't playing video games on the couch.

Hugging the bottle to his chest, Cody walked slowly around a rickety pile he was building out of the stuff he'd found. He stuck the upside-down bottle on the post of what looked like the end of a metal crib. "I'm building a mom-u...I mean, mon-u-ment."

So far his junk-pile monument was about waist high, everything balanced one thing on top of another. He pointed out Ike's dog dish, the one labeled Sparky. It sat on a bucket inside an empty picture frame. A toy truck, tires burned off, rested on its rims; Cody had parked it on top of a singed sneaker. Some things were too black or melted to identify. I know *I* wouldn't mess with this stuff even if I was wearing old clothes.

"Some of it is pretty." Cody swirled a finger along the inside of a metal curlicue. The curlicue was on one of the two heavy pieces of wrought iron he'd leaned together to hold up his monument.

Cass tossed her ponytail back over her shoulder and took a closer look. "These look like the ends of a bench. The wood slats of the seat must've burned away. If we had some wood, we could replace 'em."

I gave her a friendly shove. "Ben's rubbing off on you, girl."

That was all it took to remind her that it had been a whole eighteen hours since she'd seen her boyfriend.

She ran toward the building and I followed her. It was either that or help Cody—and my shirt was pretty new.

As Cass pushed the door open, Ben and Big looked up. They sat sneaker to sneaker in two stuffed chairs they'd turned toward each other.

"Hey." Ben looked like we'd maybe caught them talking about some kind of a secret. I knew for sure when Justin got suddenly interested in the knee of his jeans.

"What is all this?" I walked around Big's chair and over to the shelf where the old board games had been. Now it was full of food. A rolled-up Boy Scouts sleeping bag sat on top of the piano. "What's going on?"

"Just put in a few supplies," Big mumbled. "For, you know. Contingencies."

"Yeah," said Ben. "Contingencies."

Big got out of the armchair and began to pace.

I fell into his empty seat. "What kind of contingencies?" I looked at Ben and Ben looked at Big.

"Okay." Big held up both hands. "Let's say things get so bad at home—your home, my home—this goes for any of us. Anyway, say home gets so bad it goes radioactive, or implodes, then I—I mean, any one of us—could come here and hole up, now that we have the place supplied."

I hung my legs over the arm of the chair. "You won't have water or electricity."

Cass perched on the edge of Ben's chair. "Or a bathroom." So far we'd never stayed long enough to need one.

"I'm talking emergency response here, people." Justin played a nervous rhythm on the thighs of his jeans. "Remember the bomb shelters we read about in social studies? How back when Russia was about to bomb the crap out of us, people dug holes in their yards and made underground rooms where they could hang out till the radiation went away in, like, a million years? You think they worried about comfort?"

"It would be scary here at night," Cass said quietly.

He stood in the middle of the hot, dusty room, sweating. "Not as scary as it gets at my house."

"You should try talking to them," I said. Big needed to stand up to his parents, tell them how he felt.

"*You* try making them listen!" he shot back, like he'd caught my comment on the rebound. "This is just a backup plan. Those bomb shelters never got used—and this one probably won't either—but just in case, I'm set. I mean, we're set. The thing is, if one of us *does* hole up here, no one can tell anyone."

Ben tipped his head back against the seat with a quiet thump and stared at the ceiling. "If Dad asked me flat-out and I lied, I'd be grounded for life. But hey, I've been grounded for life before." He sat back up. "Cass?" he prodded. "You're in, right?"

She twisted the end of her ponytail; her dad would kill her if she lied.

But she nodded. Of course she was in. She always went along with Ben.

Justin took a deep breath, looking at me last. "Jemmie?"

I swung my legs, listening to the soft thud of my heels against the upholstery. I always thought Big exaggerated about how bad it was at home, but if camping out eating chips and cold beans and peeing in the bushes was an improvement, maybe he was telling the truth. "Sure. Why not? You'll never do it anyway." Watching him flinch, I wished I hadn't said the last part, but it was the kind of stuff I always said to Big. "Maybe I can bring out an old air mattress," I added fast.

"We'll collect jugs from the recycling bins and fill 'em." Ben sounded like he was wishing it was his parents who were about to go radioactive so he'd have an excuse to run away to the woods.

"Don't forget toilet paper," I said.

Big blushed right up to the roots of his hair.

JUStiN

Everyone is thinking about me and toilet paper when Cody wanders in, breaking the awkward silence.

"It's too hot in here," he complains.

We all think it's hot, but until Ben says it's time to go, we're here.

May as well do something till he does. I take the wet sponge I brought from home out of the Baggie and start wiping down my piano.

Cody sits on the floor with the hat beside him, pulls the stack of comics out of the sleeping bag, and begins arranging them in a circle with himself and the hat in the middle. As he puts each one down, he silently lifts the cover and shows me the name written inside, Paul Cody Floyd. I nod each time, then take another swipe at my dusty piano.

I've only got, like, half the top of the piano clean, before the sponge is totally gross. I'm using the kitchen towel on the keys when Cass opens a trunk and pulls out an armload of fabric. "Look, you guys!" She sits back on her heels.

The girls decide curtains would be a good starter project for Cass before she sews the dress. She holds up two choices of fabric, like a QVC hostess. "Do you want red curtains or blue?"

Ben and I trade glances. Curtains?

"Red or blue?" Cass repeats.

"Blue," we say together.

Cass and Jemmie hold the fabric up and stretch it across a window, measuring—turns out they'll need blue *and* red to cover all the windows. The old curtain rods still look sturdy enough.

Together they get the old sewing machine going—seems like Nana Grace has one just about as ancient. And it doesn't look like rocket science: pump the treadle and the needle goes up and down. After a while, Jemmie gets bored, but by then Cass has the hang of it.

I'm noodling around on the piano when Jemmie says, "Wonder what's in here?" I turn and see her tugging at the brass knobs on a chest of drawers with rings on top like someone put a glass of Coke on it about a million times. She leans back hard but nothing happens. "Big?"

I know she needs my weight again. Is being heavy the only thing I'm good for in Jemmie's world?

We each grab a knob. As we pull it out the drawer shrieks. "Sounded like a ghost," Cody whispers.

Startled, Cass looks up from the sewing machine. "It sure did."

"You guys ever hear of friction?" Ben asks.

I peer into the drawer, but the stuff inside just looks like more fabric, nothing scary.

Jemmie folds back the piece of cloth on top. "Tablecloth...napkins." She digs way down. "What's this?" She pulls out a paper bag. "HAPPY BIRTHDAY!" is written on it with a thick Magic Marker—definitely a guy-wrapping job.

She opens the bag and peers in. "Fireworks!" She plunges in an arm and comes up with a fistful. "Spinners. We had some of these at *your* birthday, didn't we, Ben?" She holds out a couple of the thick disks.

127

"Nah," Ben says, writing down a measurement for the extra shelves he says we need. "Spinners are too unpredictable. They take off in all directions. Dad was afraid we'd set something on fire."

Cody stares, his mouth hanging open. "Ya think a spinner landed on the house and burned it down?"

Ben bops the side of Cody's head with his palm. "Imagination overload!"

I thought about the newspaper report. All it said was the cause of the fire was "under investigation."

"It *could* have been caused by a spinner," says Cody, like he's reading my mind.

"Yeah, right. Or maybe Zeus zapped the house with a bolt of lightning," Ben jokes. Before becoming a dinosaur hunter, Cody was big into myths and legends.

"I'll find out." Cody puts on the hat and disappears under it, sitting in the middle of his comic-book circle.

Jemmie gives the bag a shake. "Wonder why they were hidden at the bottom of this drawer."

I see Cody's shoulders stiffen—the word "hidden" has got to be giving him and the hat ideas.

"Who says they were hidden?" I ask. "They were probably just stuffed in there to get them out of the way." Jemmie has obviously never been in my room.

She studies the spinners with their red and blue lightning-bolt wrappers; I study her. Tiny, damp curls stick to her forehead—she's even pretty when she sweats.

"They're probably too old to work anyway." She drops the spinners into the bag and crams the bag back in the drawer.

Cody solemnly lifts the hat off his head, his eyes wide. "Yes."

No one asks, *Yes, what?* Up until he found that hat, no one ever paid that much attention to Cody—even with the hat, they can forget about him. I notice the look on his face and the "yes," because

128

being ignored happens to me too. So, I nod at him, like, *Yes, I hear you.* Not like, *Yes, I believe a talking hat just gave you the scoop about a "Happy Birthday!" spinner that burned the house down.*

After pronouncing that "yes," Cody sets the hat down as far away as he can reach. Cass works on the curtains. I play the piano. Ben quits measuring the wall and sticks the pencil behind his ear. He and Jemmie start a game of darts.

I turn when a dart thwacks the board and notice Cody just sitting, an unopened comic in his lap.

"Hey," I say to him. "How's this for a new superhero? Super Hat!"

"Yeah," says Ben. "A superhero dedicated to curing dandruff and worldwide baldness!"

Most days Cody would think that was super funny. Today he just looks spooked.

I break out a package of Oreos. Cody says he's thirsty. Ben tells him he isn't.

It's getting hotter and hotter in the garage and we don't have anything to drink—or any toilet paper. We keep looking at Ben for a signal that it's okay to go home—he's gotta be thirsty too.

It's about two when Jemmie's pocket begins playing music. She fishes her cell out.

I can hear Nana Grace's voice. "Where are you, child?"

"I'll be right home," Jemmie answers. "Sorry, guys. Gotta go." Not looking at all sorry, she slides the phone back into her pocket.

"I'll walk you," I say, surprising everyone, especially myself. I figure they'll all want to come along—Cody sure does—but Cass says she has a couple more seams to sew on a curtain and Ben says he and Cody are sticking around for right now. Then he and Cass shoo us toward the door like they want the two of us to walk home together. So we walk out. Together. Alone.

Jemmie doesn't talk. I don't talk.

This is awkward.

She watches her feet. "Want to run again?"

"'Want' and 'run' do not belong in the same sentence."

I'm dredging my mind for some non-dumb topic when Jemmie asks, "Would you really spend the night out there in the woods?"

"I don't know," I admit. "But the constant yelling at home? It's hard to take." I hold up a hand. "And don't tell me to talk to them. I've tried, but it's like I'm not even there. I talk, but they never listen."

"My mom's not the best listener either."

Okay, she's being sympathetic, but I know she doesn't get it. "No, really. My parents take not-listening to a whole new level. Sometimes I have this nightmare where I'm talking but no sound comes out." I move my mouth like I'm shouting, then I realize that I probably look like my goldfish, Xena, blubbing silently on the other side of the aquarium glass.

I glance at Jemmie, but she's not laughing at me. I jam my hands into the pockets of my shorts. "Can I tell you something?"

Her eyes shift my way. "O-kay."

"Yesterday Butler said I have what it takes to be a musician."

I want her to say, "Way to go, Big!" I want her to be happy for me.

She watches her sneakers.

"Glad to hear it, Big," I say for her. "You definitely have the talent." I wait for her to contradict me.

She seems to be building up to it as the silence stretches. She takes a deep breath...opens her mouth...and says, "You do."

I was so expecting a put-down, I almost ask, *Do what?*

"You're good. Really, really good. But being a musician is a hard life."

Of course it is—I'd never get lucky and pick something easy.

"My dad was a musician," she went on. "He painted houses to earn money and played on the side. He was always on the phone looking for gigs, trying to catch a break. It's not enough to be good. You have to hustle."

I kick at some leaves. "Hustle, huh?"

"Yes, hustle—and even then it doesn't always work out." Her arm bumps my sweaty arm and she pulls away fast. "But the first thing you have to do if you're going to make it is believe in yourself."

We both know someone who *really* believes in himself. Suddenly I'm doing Leroy. "I'm the piano guy, and I'm gonna fly. Play arpeggios just like the pros."

"What?" She stops walking and rests her knuckles on her hips. "Leroy brags too much, but put a ball in his hands, he can back it up. He believes in himself. How about you, Big? Do you believe in yourself?"

"Yeah." I swallow hard. "Yeah, I do." I'm surprised to hear myself say it, but I think it's true when it comes to my music. "So who do I convince next?"

I want her to say, "Me." But she's not Cass, and I'm not Ben.

"Your parents, of course. Have they ever heard you play?"

"Not much," I admit. "My mom stayed for a lesson once. And, my dad? Never."

"Start there. Make them listen."

"What do I tell them? 'Put on some long pants and walk through these stickers, I have something to play for you'?"

"No. Bring them to my house. They can drink sweet tea and listen to their son. The musician."

She actually winks at me before she takes off.

Wow. That was unexpected.

thursday
(seven minus three)

CODY

Cody climbed up on a chair and wiggled a family photo album off the shelf. It was the oldest. Before him, before Ben—even before Mom. He had just opened it to the middle when his dad came down the stairs.

"Hey, Sport!"

"Hey, Dad!" His father's hair was wet from his shower, not yet pulled into a ponytail, and he was in just his drawers. His yesterday-greasy coveralls hung on a hook in the kitchen. Mom thought he should put on a clean pair every day, but Dad always said, "Why bother? Every day's grease day at the garage."

Dad pulled out a second chair. "You're up early."

"You too."

"Looking at pictures? Those are old ones, from when I was a kid. Why the sudden interest?"

Cody nodded at the hat, which sat next to a vase of Mom's roses. "Looking for Uncle Paul."

"Well, you found him." Dad pointed at a picture of two kids in swim trunks. The taller boy had his arm around the shorter one's neck.

"The big kid's strangulating the little one," Cody said, although both boys were grinning.

"They're just horsing around. Uncle Paul's the little guy.

The one with the tomahawks on his swim trunks is his best bud, Cole."

"His best bud sure is a lot bigger than he is."

"Cole was a couple years older. Paul always hung out with older kids."

"Kinda like me with Ben's friends."

"Kinda."

Cody leaned on his elbows. "Looks like they're having a good time."

"Oh, they always had a good time." Dad stared at the picture, shaking his head.

Cody's finger skipped from photo to photo. "Uncle Paul… Uncle Paul…Uncle Paul." The next three pages were full of those same kids: Uncle Paul and Cole doing a double-cannonball off the tower at Wakulla Springs. Uncle Paul and Cole standing on the peak of a roof waving their arms. Uncle Paul and Cole on bikes, each with one foot on the seat and the other leg straight out to the side.

"They called that trick 'the peeing dog,'" said Dad.

Cody snorted a laugh.

Dad folded his arms on the edge of the table and leaned in too. For someone looking at the peeing dog trick, he sure looked sad. He glanced up, then nudged the hat with one knuckle. "Still wearing this?" he asked.

"Of *course*. I'm Detective Dobbs."

"Bet your head gets hot."

"Kind of does," Cody admitted. He touched his prickly buzz-cut. "But I don't wear it all the time. Like now? I'm airing my head out."

"Good. You don't want to get athlete's head."

"What's athlete's head?"

"The same as athlete's foot, only at the other end." He waved Cody in close like he was going to tell him a secret. "It rots your brain."

"*Da-ad.*"

"All right, there's no such thing as athlete's head, but maybe you should put the hat up for now. You can take it down again when you're big enough to see out from under it."

"That's okay." Cody liked being Detective Dobbs. Ben and everybody else listened to Detective Dobbs. Nobody listened to plain old Cody. Maybe when he was seven they would. But probably not.

They heard the swish of slippers zombie-walking in the hall upstairs.

"Sudoku," they said together.

Mom would need her coffee and her puzzle to wake up her brain when she stumbled into the kitchen.

Dad looked at Cody, then down at his own tiger-striped boxers. "One of us is going to have to get the paper in his pajamas."

"Me." Cody climbed out of his chair. "Grown-ups aren't allowed outside in their pj's." Plus, the neighbors wouldn't know Dad's boxers *were* his pj's. "You do coffee." Cody jogged out the front door and jumped off the top step.

Without the hat he could see up. He watched a couple of squirrels chase each other along an oak limb, then jump to the next tree.

He was still squirrel watching when he heard a *tap-tap-tap*. On the other side of the window, Dad mouthed, *Su-do-ku.*

Sudoku. Cody trotted to the end of the driveway and looked in the green newspaper box—one time he found a bird's nest in there with two babies. Today, just a paper. He was about to reach in when he heard a voice say, "You gonna think about it?"

He peered around the mailbox. Jemmie and Leroy were walking toward him down the street. Leroy had a backpack slung over one shoulder and a basketball tucked under his arm. Seemed like they were talking serious—Cody could tell they didn't notice him. "Hi!" he called out.

Jemmie waved and gave him a big smile.

Leroy didn't look as happy to see him. "Hey, Detective Dobbs!" He popped the ball at him. It hit Cody in the chest and rolled along the gutter.

"No hat today." Cody pointed at his bare head. "So I can't catch. Like usual."

Jemmie scooped up the loose ball and dribbled it ahead of her. "You don't need a magic hat to catch a ball," she said. "You just need to practice."

Cody jogged along beside them. "Where are you guys going?"

Leroy tapped his chest with a thumb. "Summer school, though I ain't no fool, then basketball camp, where I'm the champ."

Dribbling the ball with one hand, Jemmie punched Leroy's shoulder with the other.

"Where are *you* going, Jemmie?" Cody skipped; they were moving pretty fast. "You don't have to go to summer school, and you're already a champ."

"Me?" She gave Cody a sly smile. "Nowhere."

"You're going there *now?*"

Jemmie glanced at Leroy, then raised her eyebrows at Cody. "Right now I'm walking Mr. Didn't-Study to summer school."

"Why?"

Leroy grinned. "She has the hots for me."

"You wish!" Jemmie took off, driving the ball out ahead of her.

Leroy jetted after her like the two of them were tied together with a really short rope.

"Sudoku," Cody reminded himself, and he turned around.

Justin was standing at the end of the driveway, the newspaper in his hand.

"Hey, Justin!" Cody called. "How's it goin'?"

Justin stared past him, watching the runners like he hadn't even heard the question.

Justin

After Ben's mom goes upstairs to get dressed for work, I pick up her unfinished sudoku puzzle.

I hate sudoku, but I dig right in, figuring out where to put a missing three. Doing the puzzle is like digging my nails into my palms the time I wiped out bad on my skateboard and took all the skin off both knees. A small pain can kind of distract you from a big one.

I think about how I suck at sudoku so I won't have to think about Leroy and Jemmie.

Cartoons are on in the next room. Cody laughs. I scribble in a couple of numbers. Ben stumbles into the kitchen, his eyes barely open. He peers over my shoulder and points at a seven. "That should be a nine." He's not even awake and he's better than I am at sudoku.

Ben is finishing off a broccoli quiche when his parents walk back into the kitchen. Instead of her usual flowing skirt, Mrs. Floyd wears what she calls her "office manager disguise"—a blue suit. Putting on my "happy disguise," I give her a big smile. "Have a good day," I tell her.

Mr. Floyd is in boxers, a white T-shirt, and red socks. He steps into the greasy coveralls that hang by the door and jams his feet into a pair of rotted-out Nikes.

Mrs. Floyd kisses the top of Ben's head, then mine. Before following her out the door, Mr. Floyd turns back to Ben, points a finger, and says what he says anytime he leaves Ben in charge. "No disasters."

"Same to you, Dad."

As soon as we hear the car drive off, Ben yells, "Cody? I'm fixing your cereal."

"After this cartoon."

"Pouring the milk…"

"Not yet! It'll get soggy!" Cody skids through the door. "No you're not!"

Ben shrugs. "Why would I? You're seven minus three. Do it yourself. But hurry up. We want to go to Nowhere before it gets too hot."

ை

When we get to our hideout it's silent—and I'm relieved.

Cody goes back to work on his monument.

Ben scrambles up the ladder with a hammer in his hand. Before long he'll find something to bang on, but for now he sits on the edge of the roof.

I climb up after him. Why not? The girls'll show up soon and I'll noodle around on the piano and keep my back to Jemmie, but for right now we're two guys sitting on a roof, our legs hanging.

Ben tosses the hammer from hand to hand. As it slaps his palms he looks around. "It's almost like we're in the middle of the wilderness."

A semi shifts gears out on Rankin. "Maybe not the exact middle," I say.

"Close as we're gonna get." He lies back on the roof. "You think there's real wilderness anywhere anymore?"

I'm pretty sure this is what Mr. Butler calls a "rhetorical question," which is a question you don't need to answer, like "What are you, crazy?" or "How's it going, Justin?"

Ben squints up at the dead limb over our heads. "Sooner or later that branch'll come crashing down."

I lie back on the roof too.

Ben laces his hands behind his head. "Remember the Sword of Damocles?"

"Sure, the sword dangling by a thread over the guy's head." Cody was big on that legend for a while. I think he just liked saying "Damocles."

Big as it is, the limb we're lying under is nothing compared to the other swords I have hanging over my head.

"Cody's awful quiet," says Ben. "I wonder what he's up to?" But he doesn't bother to look.

I prop up on an elbow. Below, at the edge of the clearing, Cody is standing on his toes balancing something on top of his monument. "That stack of stuff is beginning to look dangerous. Nothing is attached to anything else. It's, like, the Junk Pile of Damocles."

"Cody's not much of a tool user."

"He wouldn't mess with that stuff if he knew what happened to the family who owned it." I lie back down. "Speaking of that, I thought we'd at least tell the girls."

"I did too," Ben admits. "I meant to, sometime when Cody wasn't around, but Cass was so relieved. Now if we told them it would be like we lied."

"I thought you told Cass everything."

"Not everything."

I fold my hands on my chest and stare past the dead branch at a hot blue sky. "I kind of think we should tell them." I glance over at him. "Cass is sewing a dead girl's dress. Didn't it kind of creep you out when she tried it on?"

"We can't bring Lucy Branson back, Jus, and it's not like she died wearing that dress. Why screw things up by telling? We *all* need this place."

All is an exaggeration. He needs it. I need it. The rest of us would be happier somewhere else. Jemmie, for instance, would rather be with Leroy.

Ben sighs. "I could fall asleep up here."

Me too. The warm roof feels good through my T-shirt, just like the road did when I had that delusion Jemmie might like me.

Down below, I hear someone coming, crunching through the leaves. "Hey, Ben!"

He sits up. "Hey, Cass."

When I lift my head, Cass is standing on the bottom rung of the ladder. Jemmie's on the ground behind her. "Can I come up?" Cass calls.

Me, Ben, and Cass on the roof together? Awk-ward. "Hold on. Let me come down first."

Also awkward—Jemmie watching my big butt come down that ladder.

But I make it to the ground and we both watch Cass scramble up.

She parks herself real close to Ben on the edge of the roof, the white soles of her sneakers flashing as she swings her legs back and forth. They hold hands.

I stuff my hands in my pockets. "This reminds me of the black-and-white movies my mom likes."

Jemmie looks at me like I might be crazy. "Yeah? How?"

"There are the stars and then there are their goofy friends—they're what's called 'comic relief.'"

She glances up at the hand-holders on the roof. "I guess we're the goofy friends."

"We're for sure not the stars." Then I think of a different movie,

the one that played first thing this morning. Jemmie and Leroy, running down the street together. In that one they'd be the stars.

Me, on the sidewalk with my mouth hanging open?

Comic relief. Definitely.

Jemmie

With Cass and Ben on the roof and Cody building his monument, that left me and Big. I challenged him to a game of Monopoly.

He didn't have to do a thing but roll the dice and move his token.

I stood on the rickety chair and dug the Monopoly box out of the pile on the shelf.

I wiped off the dust and set up the board. I even let him choose his token first—he chose the boot. This was a really old-time Monopoly game.

"Your turn," I said now, putting the dice in his hand for, like, the fifth time. All he had to do was drop them. I waited, listening to the *thunk* of Cass swinging her heels against the side of the building. That girl had it easy.

She didn't have Leroy bugging her to "think about it."

She wasn't playing a stupid board game with Big, wondering why, for one second, she'd almost liked him. "Could you just take your turn before we both die of old age?"

He sighed, and the dice plopped out of his hand. One rolled under the edge of a dresser. I slid it out and added the two together. "Nine."

The boot limped along until it landed on the question mark of Chance.

"Here." I handed him the top card.

He read it and shook his head. "Figures."

"What figures?"

He handed it back to me.

"'Go to jail, go directly to jail. Do not pass go. Do not collect two hundred dollars.'" I put the card back at the bottom of the pile. "Good. At least now I won't have to remind you to roll the dice for a couple turns."

"Take three turns!" He doubled his slump. "Take four! Build yourself a motel."

"That's *hotel*." I rolled a seven and picked up my race car. "And don't just park there on Chance. Put your sorry self in Jail!"

He shoved the boot, which lay on its side, onto Jail.

I made my move all right. I bought Ventnor Avenue, then rolled again and bought myself a second railroad.

"I saw you this morning," he said, his bangs falling over his eyes. "With Leroy."

"You did? Why didn't you say hi?"

"You were moving pretty fast and you looked…busy."

"So…we were just getting some exercise."

"So…do you like him?"

"Leroy?" I rolled the dice and raced my car to Free Parking, then shrugged. "I like him to shoot hoops with."

He shook his bangs out of his eyes. "Not *that* kind of like."

I let the dice drop onto the board. "It sure is hot in here."

His eyes widened like he didn't know where that came from, but he went along, probably glad I changed the subject. "It's always hot in here."

"Seems hotter today," I said.

"Yeah. Today it's like a preview of hell."

"You shouldn't joke about stuff like that."

He shrugged. "It's my job to joke."

I pushed to my feet. "I'm going home. I need a glass of sweet tea." He could come along and play an in-tune piano if he wanted to, but he had to ask. I was tired of telling him to make a move.

I ambled to the door, waiting for him to say something about how he could use a glass of sweet tea too, but the door banged shut behind me without even a goodbye.

"See ya!" I yelled up to Cass on the roof.

"Jemmie?" she called after me. "I need your help finishing the dress!"

"It's coming along fine!" I yelled back. I was out of there.

"Hey! Where're you going?" Cody had a rusty horseshoe in one hand. His monument looked like it was about to topple.

"Somewhere else."

I jogged a little ways, then slowed to a walk. It was too hot to run, and I didn't want to run anyway.

I heard the out-of-tune piano plinking in the garage. Big was playing something minor and sad, but whose fault was that? All he had to say was, "A glass of sweet tea sounds good. Got one for me too?"

Leroy sure didn't have any trouble asking for things. He asked all the time.

Suddenly, I was glad this was our "last summer."

I thought about all the kids I hadn't met yet, and I liked them already.

CODY

Cody watched Jemmie leave. Cass next. Now Justin was walking over like he wanted to look at the monument—then he'd probably leave too. Everyone was drizzling out, but Cody could hear Ben banging on something inside. That meant Ben wouldn't drizzle out and neither would he. They'd be hot by themselves together.

Partway over to the monument, Justin bent down and scooped something up. "Hey, Cody, wanna add this?" And there it was again. The burned-up doll head. Cody stuck it between a bucket and a mixing bowl where it was hard to see.

Justin flopped down at the edge of the concrete foundation. Maybe he wasn't leaving after all. Cody hoped not.

"Hey, Justin. Look what *I* found." He picked up a blackened spoon and crawled over to Justin. "Look how the handle is a loop."

"It's a baby spoon," Justin said.

"And see? It's got something written on it." Cody rubbed it with his thumb. "Starts with an *L*. Looks like it says…Lucky."

"Lucky?" Justin squinted at the writing, then he closed his eyes. "That's Lucy."

"Lucky Lucy." Cody sat back on his heels. "Was she in the article about the fire?"

"Yeah, she was." Justin blew out his breath and looked away.

"I'm beginning to think...maybe you shouldn't be messing with this."

Cody shrugged. "Why not? It's like digging for dinosaurs at home, only here I find things." He crawled back over to the pile and grabbed a necklace he'd hung from a bench curlicue. "You think this was Lucy's too?" The heart on the chain spun as he carried it over.

Justin flinched. "Geez, would you put that down?"

"Why?" The chain slid off his finger and the heart plunked onto Justin's knee.

Justin swatted it away. "Would you quit messing with this stuff, Cody? I'm serious."

"But why?"

Justin stared off toward the garage like he was listening to the hammer, then he turned back and got real close to Cody. "Because..." he whispered. "Lucy didn't make it out of the fire. She died." Just then the hammer stopped. "Oh crap! Ben's gonna kill me."

As the hammering started again, Cody turned toward his monument, wide-eyed. "Lucy...died?"

"And she wasn't the only one."

"How..." Cody gulped. "How many people got killed?"

"Three. Lucy and both her parents."

"What about Ike?"

"Ike?" Justin dragged his hand down his hot, red face. "Ike? Oh yeah, the dog. The article didn't mention any dog."

"But Ben said they all got out." Cody's voice felt shaky.

"He didn't want to give you nightmares. And he didn't want to give this place up."

Cody knew right away that was the real reason.

"Besides, even if we never came back it wouldn't change anything."

"But…everyone died," Cody said, staring at his sooty hands.

"Not everyone. There was a kid named Coleman. He got out."

Cody startled. The peeing dog! For a few seconds he just sat, breathing through his mouth. "Can I ask you a question?"

"You can ask, but that's all I know, and Ben is going to kill me for telling you."

"If your name was Coleman, what do you think people would call you for a nickname?"

Justin looked surprised. "Why ask that?"

"Just wondering."

"I dunno." Justin shoved his legs out straight, digging grooves in the damp leaves with his heels. "Cole? Yeah, probably Cole."

Cody nodded once. "Thought so."

"You are one weird little dude, Cody." Justin glanced again at the garage. "And I am so dead."

"No you're not." Cody put on the hat, balancing it on his ears. "Detective Dobbs won't tell Ben. That's why there's a 'private' in 'private eye.'"

Justin looked sort of relieved, but not all the way. "I know you'll try, but sometimes your mouth engages before your brain."

"I'm not gonna tell him, for really." Cody turned and looked at his monument, then rubbed his sooty hands on his shorts. "All this stuff belongs to *dead* people."

Justin looked too. "You know, most monuments are to dead people, so maybe building this one's okay. It's like you're honoring them."

Cody picked up the necklace that lay on the slab by its thin chain. He was about to hang it back on a bench curlicue when he glanced at the hat and knew—as if the hat had told him—he should take the necklace with him. He hesitated. What if he got caught breaking the rule about not taking stuff from Nowhere? But Justin was staring at the ground between his sneakers. Looking at the hat again, Cody took a deep breath, and even though he didn't want to mess with anything from the fire ever again, he shoved the necklace into the pocket of his shorts.

He and Justin both jumped when a door closed. "Hot enough for you guys?" Ben was standing in front of the garage, his T-shirt soaked with sweat.

"Hot enough times two," Cody yelled back.

"What are you waiting for, an invitation? Let's get us some lunch."

"Reprieve," Justin muttered under his breath as Ben walked away into the trees. "Remember, Dobbs." He zipped his fingers across his lips—and Cody zipped back.

☙

Afraid he'd blab, Cody didn't engage his mouth all the way home. After lunch, he figured they'd all head back to the garage in the woods. He didn't want to, now that he knew the ghosts he'd felt as tingles were real. But Ben didn't mention going to Nowhere. Justin didn't either. Instead, the two of them started playing video games. For once Cody didn't try to pester his way into the game.

He had more important things to do. Detective work.

Like he had earlier that day, he pulled a chair over to the shelf with the photo albums on it. He climbed up and grabbed the same album, the one with the peeing dog trick in it. He walked it to the kitchen table and set it down next to the hat.

This time he started at the beginning.

"Baby pictures..." He looked through a few pages. "Bare butts in the tub. Gross!"

He kept going and found Dad, a chubby kid in cutoff jean shorts with his skinny little brother on his shoulders. Cody picked up the album for a better look. Uncle Paul had a cartoon Band-Aid on his knee. "Tweety Bird," he said.

Cody flipped through lots of Christmases—Uncle Paul sitting on a bike with a big bow on the handlebars. G-mom and G-dad sitting next to the tree, smiling. It took a second to recognize G-dad with hair.

He came to where Uncle Paul was in Little League, then, taller and older, in Babe Ruth league. And finally Cody was back to the photos Dad had looked at with him.

He turned to the next page and sucked in his breath. He looked closer. So close he almost put his nose on the yellowed photo.

He pulled back. Blinked. Looked again. He got a magnifier out of the jar on Mom's desk, but the picture stayed the same. His neck prickled, like the ghosts from the fire were there in the room with him. He slid a hand into his pocket and touched the necklace.

He had to do something, show someone, ask someone what to do. But who?

Not Ben, for sure. Justin? Maybe, but he didn't seem to know what was right and wrong unless Ben told him. Mom and Dad would know, but he wasn't allowed to even *think* about this stuff around them.

He needed to ask someone what to do. He thought of Cass. Even though Ben could sometimes talk her into things, she knew what was right and what was wrong.

He slid the album into his old school pack and grabbed the hat. "Going to Cass's."

Ben didn't even glance up from the screen. "Tell her to send you home when she gets tired of you—and don't go throwing sand at Missy."

Cody's pack felt extra heavy as he trudged over to the Bodines'.

Jemmie

L ong as you two are just sitting around," Nana Grace said, "you might as well make yourselves useful."

"Useful" meant shelling peas for supper.

Easiest way to shell peas according to my grandmother is to put a mess of them in your lap and plunk the shelled peas into a pot between your feet. But to have a lap to put the peas in, you have to wear a skirt. Since Cass and me were wearing shorts, Nana tied a flowered apron around each of us.

We were sitting side by side on the porch swing shelling peas when Cody and the hat walked toward us across the lawn. The school pack hanging off his skinny shoulders looked heavy.

Cass plinked a couple of peas in the pot and called out, "Hey, Cody!"

"Hi." For Cody, who usually crowed his hellos, this one was awful quiet. "I was going to see you at your house but you weren't there," he told Cass.

"No, I'm here."

"Got something to show you." He climbed the porch stairs and carefully set the hat on the top step. His bony knees hit the floor and he slid a big old photo album out of his pack. He hugged it to his chest and looked back and forth between us.

"So show us," I said. Not that I was interested in old pictures, but I was pretty tired of shelling peas.

Cass slid over, making a space between us on the porch swing for Cody.

He sat and opened the album to page one and began showing us pictures of his dad and his missing uncle as little kids. Cass said how cute Cody's dad was, his brother too.

I yawned. Family pictures were about as interesting as shelling peas. Then I noticed how Cody seemed to be getting more nervous each time he turned the page. "This is Uncle Paul and his best friend, Coleman. Cole for short. Cole was a couple of years older."

The boys in the pictures were having a good old time, riding bikes and swimming.

Cass pointed out a picture of the boys doing a double-jump off the tower at Wakulla Springs. "We do that!"

"Every chance we get," I said. "Wish we were there right now."

Cody turned the page again. "Notice anything about this picture?" He prodded a photo of the same two guys and a girl sitting on a bench.

I couldn't figure out what he wanted us to notice. "They're getting older," I said.

Cass held back her hair. "About our age. The girl looks sort of like Cole."

I checked it out. Her hair was brown and wavy like his. Their smiles made their eyes crinkle in the same way. I noticed that the girl was skinny like Cass.

"That's Cole's sister, Lucy." Cody's voice was hushed.

Cass shoved the swing gently with her toes. "She looks like a Lucy." The swing stopped as Cass bent over the page. "Is she holding hands with your uncle?"

Cody nodded. "Yup."

Didn't look like it to me. I brought my face so close I could smell the musty page. "You sure?"

"They are, for really. I checked with my mom's magnifier."

"Like a real detective, huh?"

He sat up straight. "I *am* a real detective."

"I guess Lucy was your uncle's girlfriend." I could hear the smile in Cass's voice—she was really into the boyfriend-girlfriend thing. "I like her necklace."

"Want to see it?" Cody dug in the pocket of his shorts. The chain came out first, hooked on his finger, then the heart. The chain was a smoky gray, the sparkle in the middle of the heart dulled.

"How come you have it?" Cass asked.

"Found it in the leaves by my monument."

Cass and I stared at each other, then back at the necklace.

"It was *their* house that burned down?" Cass glanced at the photo and her eyes widened. "Oh my gosh, the bench!" She put her finger on the twisted metal curlicues in the picture.

We'd all seen the ends of that bench. They weren't green anymore. They were charred black, and they were holding up Cody's monument.

"Good thing they all got out of the fire," Cass said. "I wonder if Cole and his sister are still in Pittsburgh."

Cody sat between us like a stone. He didn't move, he didn't breathe. I put my feet down flat, stopping the swing. "What is it, Cody? Spill."

"Something I'm not supposed to tell. I promised Justin."

"A promise to Big doesn't count." I was joking, but that was all Cody needed.

"Lucy's dead!" he blurted. "She didn't get out. And…and…neither did their parents. Only Cole was okay 'cause he wasn't in the house during the fire."

"But…but the guys found it in the newspaper article." Cass

sounded confused. "Ben said everyone got out. Even the dog."

I wasn't confused, but I kept my mouth shut. Let Cody do the explaining.

"Ben didn't exactly tell the truth." He fidgeted. "He…sort of… lied."

"He wouldn't lie to me," Cass said. But I could tell from her voice that she wasn't so sure.

"He did, this one time. He figured it wouldn't hurt anything. Like he says, everybody would still be dead whether we were there or not."

Cass stood up, knocking over her pot of peas. Some rolled along the cracks between the floorboards.

"Where are you going?" Cody squeaked.

"To talk to Ben."

"No!" He grabbed her hand and hung on. "Please, Cass, don't. The guys'll kill me." Still holding her arm, he went limp. She walked a couple of steps, dragging him. "If you tell them, I'll be dead too."

Any other time it would have been funny, but Cass was shook up bad. If there were rules for being a boyfriend, Ben had broken a big one. Maybe *the* big one.

Cass sat back down, real slow. Then she slumped over, picked up the edge of her flowery apron, and cried into it.

friday
(seven minus two)

Cass

Lou Anne hovered over my bed. "Are you *ever* getting up?" She was still in her nightgown, but she'd already done her hair—I knew because I'd listened to the dryer run while I pretended to be asleep. "Come on, Cass! You can't lie around all day."

I pulled the pillow over my head. I always get up way before my sister, usually right about when Mama and Daddy leave for work—but I didn't want to get up now or ever. I listened to my sister scuff down the stairs and hoped she'd leave me alone.

Ben let me make Lucy's dress, even said it looked nice when I slipped it on over my shirt and jeans. He knew that the girl who started sewing that dress had burned to death, but he didn't tell me. He'd let me put that dress on, and I couldn't even talk to him about it or I'd get Cody in trouble.

Lou Anne's slippers shushed back up the steps. "Cass?" Her voice was soft, maybe being nice, maybe just trying not to wake up Missy in the next room. "Brought you something."

When I opened my eyes, she was holding out a bowl of Lucky Charms. "Here."

I sat up in bed and took the bowl.

"Now tell me what's wrong. Something about Benji, I bet."

"How do you know it's about Ben?" Ben hated to be called Benji.

She fluffed her hair. "What else would it be about?"

Lou Anne thinks everything is about hair or guys—and she knew I didn't care about hair. She sat down on the very edge of her bed opposite me. "So…talk. Maybe I can help."

Mama says I got the brains and Lou got the looks. I don't think either one of us considers that a compliment, but being pretty, and older, my sister has a lot more experience with guys. Maybe she could help. But I couldn't talk about Ben, not without telling her everything. I tapped the spoon on the edge of the bowl, trying to decide.

"Come on, Cass…. You know you want to tell me."

Actually, I did. "Okay. But you can't tell Mama and Daddy."

"Of course I won't."

That was one good thing about Lou. It wouldn't be the first time she'd kept a secret from our parents.

Still, I made her pinkie swear, and then I told her about Nowhere and the fire and Ben letting me put on a dead girl's dress. Her eyes kept getting wider and she kept interrupting with Lou questions like, "Isn't it buggy in that woods?" and "Where do you go to the bathroom?"

I told her to focus on the Ben part, then I asked for her advice.

While she thought, I finished my soggy cereal—I'd given her a lot to think about.

We sat on our beds, our nighties pulled down over our knees and tucked under our feet. She was still thinking and I was drinking the last of the milk in the bowl when someone knocked on our front door. I took a quick peek out our bedroom window. "Shoot, Lou, it's Ben! You get it."

"No way! You think I want your boyfriend to see me in my nightie? What would Daddy say?"

"What would Daddy say if Ben saw me in mine?" I held my folded hands up to her, begging. "And I can't talk to him now. You haven't told me what to do."

"True."

The knock came again.

"Oh, all right." She looked down, then wrapped herself in her bedspread. Dragging it behind her, she padded down the stairs.

I closed the door, but not all the way.

I heard the front door open and Ben's voice. "I know it's kind of early, but is Cass around? Figured we'd shoot hoops or something before it gets really hot."

"She's still in bed, Benji." Which wasn't a lie.

I heard the front door close. I expected Lou Anne and her bedspread cape to trail back into the room, and then she'd tell me what to do, but she didn't come back. I looked around the edge of the door. "Lou?"

Downstairs was awful quiet. I stepped into my shorts, pulled a T-shirt over my head, then caught myself in the mirror on my sister's vanity. My hair was all flat on one side and Lou hadn't even mentioned it.

She must've really been feeling sorry for me.

I opened the bedroom door quietly, then hung over the stair rail. When I didn't hear anything, I snuck, barefoot, down the stairs.

No Lou in the kitchen. No Lou anywhere.

"Lu-Lu?" I looked up and my little sister was calling from the top of the stairs, dragging her bunny, Flop, by one ear. Her reddish hair looked slept-on too.

I held out my arms in a big shrug—Missy likes everything big. "I don't know where Lu-Lu is, Missy, but I'm here." When she opened her arms too, I loped up the steps and carried her down on my hip.

I sat Missy in her chair and gave her a bowl of cereal too. She knocked over her juice. I was under the table mopping it up when the front door opened again and Lou Anne came in, trailing her blanket and holding her head high like a queen or something.

I stood up with the wet sponge in my hand, about to ask her where she'd been all that time when I saw Ben flash by outside the window, running down the street. Orange juice was dripping on the kitchen floor, but I didn't care. "What did you do, Lou?"

She draped her bedspread over a kitchen chair, then pulled a baby comb out of the drawer by the sink and ran it through Missy's hair. "I just talked to him."

My heart raced. "About what?"

She waved her free hand. "About, you know, everything."

"But we pinkie swore…"

She stopped combing. "To not tell Mama and Daddy, right?" She must have seen how scared I looked, but she just waved the hand holding the comb. "Listen, Cass. This is what girls do for each other. They smooth things out. I know, Jemmie's your best friend." She touched herself in the middle of the chest with the comb. "I'm just your sister. But Jemmie doesn't know about smoothing things out with a boyfriend. She doesn't even have one."

"But if you told him everything, you got Justin and Cody in trouble too."

Lou's eyes widened. "Shoot. I forgot." She fished a couple of barrettes out of the jar and put the comb back in. "I was concentrating on you and Ben. That's the important thing."

"What did he say?"

She snapped a pink pony barrette into Missy's hair. "He said he'd meant to tell you, but it was never the right time."

I leaned toward her, going up on my toes. "And *you* said?"

"And *I* said it's always the right time to tell your girlfriend the truth."

"And *he* said?"

"And *he* said something about killing those guys," she admitted.

"*Killing* them?"

She held up a hand. "So, it didn't go *exactly* the way I planned."

Even though Ben was long gone, she stared out the window like she was watching him run down the street, then turned to me. "My best advice? Give it a rest. Let him miss you." She held up one finger. "I guarantee he will, Cass, and then he'll come begging."

Begging? Lou Anne didn't know Ben very well if she thought that.

She put her hands on her thighs and leaned down to Missy. "Good morning, baby girl! What are we going to do today?" Lou got all carried away, fussing over Missy and baby-talking her like she hadn't just wrecked my life.

I didn't cry till I got out of the house and sat down in the old rocker behind the bush. I put my head down on my knees and sobbed.

I could hear water spraying next door. I thought it was covering my crying until a voice yelled, "Hey!" from the other side of the fence. I jerked my head up and Jemmie's brown eye was looking at me through the knothole.

I wiped my nose on my arm. "What're you doing?"

"Watering." A spray of water jetted over the fence, falling on me and my chair. I heard the squeak of a faucet being turned off, then her eye was back at the hole in the fence. "You having yourself a pity party for one, or would you like some company?"

I took a shaky breath. "Guess I could use a little company."

"Coming around!" she yelled.

Holding in a sob, I listened to the soft slap of sneakers as she ran along her side of the fence.

justin

Ben's got this branch in his hand and he's slashing it back and forth ahead of him like he's mad at everything. As Cody and I follow him I wonder, did Cody leak? But when I cut my eyes toward him, Cody does the zipper-lips thing, so I guess he didn't tell.

This morning, Cody really didn't want to go to the hangout so he dragged his feet and gave Ben a hard time; maybe that's it. Or maybe it's because the predicted high today is ninety-eight degrees and it's getting there fast.

Best-case scenario? Ben will take the problem, whatever it is, up on the roof and commune with it solo—pound in a few nails or maybe rip a few out—and Cody'll look at his uncle's comics and I'll play the piano and wish it was in tune.

Maybe as his best friend I should ask what's going on, but living with my parents I've learned that sometimes not knowing is a good thing.

I'm thinking I've dodged it, but when we get inside Ben turns on us. "You guys," he says, and I know that us guys are in trouble. "You just couldn't keep your mouths shut."

Cody and I look at each other like, *Hey, it wasn't me.* But it must've been one of us—and by that I mean him. Not counting the fact I leaked to him, I've kept my mouth completely shut. Still, we both turn back to Ben like we don't have a clue what he's talking about—which is usually a good policy.

"So, Jus." Ben zeroes in on me. "You *had* to tell Cody?"

I shrug, like maybe it's a possibility.

"And *you*—Detective Dobbs—you had to go and tell Cass!"

"What?" I whip around toward Cody.

"I couldn't talk to Mom and Dad 'cause of rule number three," he says. "I had to talk to *someone*."

Ben jabs his own chest with his thumb. "You could've talked to me."

Cody blinks. "No, I couldn't. That would've gotten Justin in trouble."

"Thanks for not getting me in trouble," I mumble.

My best friend glares at me. "We'll talk about that later. Cody, why did you tell Cass?"

"I wasn't *telling* her. I was asking her what to do. What if there are bones out there? What if I find the dead people?"

I can tell he's really upset because he starts to hiccup—which is kind of good because it breaks the tension. Even Ben finds it hard to stay mad when there's a *hic* every five seconds.

"I didn't mean to—*hic*—tell! And I only told Cass and Jemmie."

"This is just great." Ben throws himself into a stuffed chair. "By now I bet everyone knows."

"How do *you* know?" I ask. "I mean about the general leakage. Did Cass tell you?"

"You kidding? I got a good talking-to from her sister about how 'honesty is the best policy' and how Cass 'deserved to know the truth.'" He rolls his eyes.

I sit backwards on the piano bench facing him. "Maybe you should've told her. She's your girlfriend."

Ben groans and rests his neck against the back of the chair.

I reach behind me and doodle a few notes on the piano, but

this isn't the time, so I quit. "On the other hand, if you had told her, we'd be hanging around your living room trying to figure out what to do for the rest of the summer."

"Right! True! I did it for her too."

I can tell he's getting less mad at us. Ben doesn't hold a grudge for long.

I guess Cody knows it too. The *hics* are getting further apart. He wanders away, sits on the sleeping bag, and begins arranging the comics on the floor again, spreading out his choices. He pauses to put the hat on, then goes back to arranging.

Ben is staring at the ceiling when I ask, "Are you and Cass still… you know…you and Cass?"

"Not sure. Lou Anne says I need to talk to her. Fine. I can talk to Cass, but what am I supposed to say?"

"Didn't her sister give you a clue?"

"She said I had to be honest with her and explain why I did it and how I would never do anything like that again." He makes his voice high and prissy, doing Lou Anne. "And how I had to promise that she could trust me from now on."

"Are you gonna?"

"I don't know how to say all that!"

"How about if Lou Anne says it for you?"

"I already asked." He stands up and swings his arms. "Looks like for now this place is guys only."

Cody pushes the hat back. "Am I a guy, Ben?"

"Half a guy."

"How about when I'm seven?"

I would've given Cody a birthday promotion—at least to three-quarters—but Ben's still in a rotten mood.

"Half," he says.

"It's pretty hot in here," Cody whines. "I feel all sweaty. Wish we had 'lectricity."

"Or a *really* long extension cord," I say. Sometimes I can joke Ben out of a bad mood.

Not this time. This time Ben tells us we're both complainers and walks out. A second later, through the window, I see him scramble up the rickety ladder and hear him step onto the roof.

I wipe my face with the front of my T-shirt. It comes away all sweaty.

"You think we can talk Ben into letting us go home?" Cody asks softly.

"No." I glance down at the comics, all those guys in tight, shiny outfits. "How do they do it? Those guys never sweat."

"They *can't* sweat. They're superheroes."

I point at a random cover. "Nice muscles."

Cody kneels up for a better look. "Of *course* he has nice muscles! He's Superman." He turns the comic his way. "You think anyone could have muscles like that in real life?"

"I doubt it. They don't even look real. You know how you can make poodles and things out of balloons?"

"Sure."

"Superman looks kind of like a balloon trick, doesn't he?"

"No, Justin. Those muscles are for real. He's Superman!" But he takes another look at the bulging arms.

"You sure? I bet that under the blue spandex is a whole bag of blown-up balloons," I say. "Pop them and Superman is just a skinny little guy who probably looks a lot like you."

Cody blinks up at me. "Ya think?"

"Sure. Let your hair grow, do the curl thing on your forehead, and you're there." I take another swipe at my face with my shirt. "You know what we need? A servant."

He thumbs the hat back, rebalancing it on his forehead. "A servant for what?"

"To fan us with one of those big palm-frond thingies." He stares at me a second, then grabs the Superman comic and waves it at my sweaty face. I've barely felt the first puff of air when a matchbook slides out from between the pages. It lands on the floor in front of him. He gasps, staring at it.

"You okay, Cody?"

"Matches!"

"Yup, those are matches."

"What if they're the ones that started the fire?"

"Your imagination is running away with you, Superman Junior."

He lets the hat fall over his face—inside the hat is Cody's personal Fortress of Solitude.

He's under there long enough for me to wonder how he can stand being in there with his own hot breath. "Hey, time to quit breathing carbon dioxide." When I lift the hat, his forehead is crinkled, his eyes squinched. "What is it, Cody?"

He opens his eyes, stunned. "The hat says those are Uncle Paul's matches."

"Makes sense. They were in his comic book."

"But why did he *need* matches?"

"He was probably trying out smoking and he didn't want anyone to know."

"Maybe…" He doesn't look convinced.

I grab the hat and put it on. Of course my whole head doesn't disappear, but I squeeze my eyes shut and act like I'm concentrating really hard.

I can feel Cody's breath on my face as he leans toward me. "What's the hat telling you?"

"The hat says…these matches belonged to your uncle, but they have no connection to the fire. He used them for cigarettes…and candles…and stuff like that."

"You made that up!" He snatches the hat back with a lot more force than I expect. "To you this is just a plain old hat, but it isn't!"

165

He sits under the hat for a while more, then I hear a loud *hic.* "Justin." His voice is a whisper. "These are the matches."

"The matches?"

"Yeah. You know, the ones that started the fire."

"Why would they be inside a comic book?"

"Because—*hic*—Uncle Paul hid them there." He lifts the hat and points to the name on the corner of the cover.

"Why would your uncle have *the* matches, Cody? And why would he hide them?"

"Because…" Cody looked scared. "He didn't *mean* to…but—*hic*—Uncle Paul burned the house down."

jemmie

The chains on the porch swing creaked as I pushed it back and forth with my bare toes. Cass sat limp beside me. To cheer her up I'd brought her a big bowl of ice cream, but it sat in her lap, the fudge ripple getting soupy.

After a while I moved the bowl to my own lap and picked up the spoon.

"How could Lou Anne do that?" she asked.

"She thought it would help." Lou Anne wasn't the brightest bulb, but she wasn't mean. "The real question is, why didn't Ben tell you the truth in the first place?"

"He knew it would upset me."

I held up the drippy spoon and looked at her. *"And?"*

"And...I might have told someone and we wouldn't have been able to go there anymore."

While I ate her ice cream she stared up at the porch ceiling my grandmother had painted heavenly blue—Nana Grace believes in blue skies even if you have to make them for yourself.

"I don't get Ben anymore," Cass said. "He's changing."

"We all are."

"Not me." She pulled her feet up and sat cross-legged on the swing.

"Sure you are." I thought about the Cass I met a couple of years ago. "You're taller." I poked her with an elbow. "And even skinnier."

"I don't *feel* different."

She did, even if she didn't know it. Used to be, running and our friendship were the most important things. "Could you just forget about Ben for a while? You have plenty to look forward to, with or without Ben Floyd. High school. A real track team." I pushed the swing hard, making the chains squeak louder.

"But I *like* him. I always have, probably from about the time I was five. Six or seven, anyway." She gazed down the street. "I wish he'd apologize."

"Just forget it! This boyfriend-girlfriend thing is more trouble than it's worth."

"Not most of the time. You'll get a boyfriend; then you'll see."

I set the empty ice cream bowl down on the porch floor with a clatter. "Maybe I will and maybe I won't."

"Jemmie? Is there any guy you actually like? I mean…that way?"

I slid down and rested my neck against the hard edge of the seat back and stared at Nana's blue sky. In a few seconds it was replaced by Cass's blue eyes looking down at me. "Jemmie, is there?"

I shrugged.

The blue eyes got all wide. "Who?"

I shrugged again. If we were the Jemmie and Cass we used to be, I would've told her in a heartbeat.

"Okay, don't tell me." She sounded disappointed but didn't push.

We didn't use to have secrets, and we were way too good friends to be polite. Ben wasn't the only one who was changing, no matter what Cass said.

Suddenly, she laughed and pointed. My big old orange tomcat, General Lee, who never changed except to get fatter, was licking the ice cream bowl—and I remembered what Big had said about comic relief.

Nana came out and asked us if we planned to moon around all day, because if we did she had some windows that needed washing. We got off the porch and started walking, but we couldn't go to Nowhere since the guys were probably there. Instead we found ourselves back at the place we'd walked to together most days for two years. Monroe Middle.

Leroy was somewhere inside, trying to multiply fractions, but the windows that faced the track were empty. Even though we'd walked over slowly, we were way too hot. Cass's freckled cheeks were bright pink.

There was a little shade right next to the school. We stood with the toes of our sneakers jammed against the brick wall and rested our foreheads on the cool window glass. "Third period algebra," I said, peering into a classroom.

"The desks sure look small," Cass puffed.

"The room too."

"We were in that class just last week," she added. "There's my desk." Our desks were together at the start of the year, but we talked too much and I got moved. I stared at the desk that had been mine—and then the one right behind it. Big's.

Cass cupped her hands above her eyes and peered through the glass. "We'll never be inside this box again."

"Not unless they have class reunions for middle school." Still, for a second I imagined Big twenty years from now, sitting in that small desk at a reunion. Would everyone know his name because of his music, or would he be just a guy working in some fast-food place wearing a paper hat?

Cass turned and slid her back down the wall until she was sitting on the ground. "Maybe I could talk to Justin."

I slid down too. "About what?"

"Ben." She glanced at me like she was hoping I'd say it was a great idea. When I didn't, she let out a sigh. "Maybe you're better off without a boyfriend."

I sang out, "Amen, sister!" and lifted my palms the way Nana Grace does when she really agrees with someone.

Cass stared at our legs stretched out in front of us; from the knees down they were in the sun. She bumped my ankle with hers. "We need to shave our legs."

"Big-time."

She bumped my ankle again. "It used to be easier when it was just you and me, wasn't it? Jemmie and Cass, the girls who liked to run."

"Chocolate Milk." It sounded silly saying it now, but that's what we called our running team of two when we became best friends the summer before seventh. I wiggled my toes; since we weren't going to Nowhere, we both wore flip-flops. "After we shave we should paint our toenails."

She wiggled her toes too. "What color?"

Lou Anne had every color in the universe and she didn't mind sharing. "I'm thinking purple." Purple was our favorite.

"Not everything has to change, does it?"

"Like what?"

"Like purple nail polish and us being best friends."

"No, we'll always be best friends with purple toenails. Except on the track, where we'll still have purple toenails, but I'll beat you if it's a sprint."

"And I'll beat you if it isn't," she said. "Wonder what the competition will be like at Leon."

"Tougher."

"That's okay, we're tough."

"Super tough."

She stared across the raggedy grass at the dusty track we'd run so many times, a plaque with our names on it should be wired to the fence. I stared too. It felt the same as looking into our old classroom. Monroe Middle was a place we didn't belong anymore.

Suddenly she smiled. "Hey, running for Leon? Maybe we'll win gold at State."

saturday
(seven minus one)

ben

I woke up to the sound of Mom singing in the kitchen. "'Almost heaven, West Virginia...'" Everything was great in *her* world.

Pulling on my jeans, I looked out the window. It had rained all night with lots of thunder and lightning, but now the sun was out and birds were chirping, all happy. As I slouched down the stairs Dad started to whistle.

"Could you all quit it with the cheerfulness?" I said as I walked in the kitchen. "It's too early."

Dad raised his eyebrows. "Good morning to you too, Bud." Mom kept right on singing about West Virginia while she worked on her sudoku.

"Forgot your shirt," said Cody, looking up from his boring bowl of cereal. "And I can see your drawers."

When I didn't smile, he got it. This was not the day to mess with me.

As he dipped up another spoonful of soggy cereal, I thought about our walk home from Nowhere yesterday, how he kept insisting that the hat said Uncle Paul had burned the house down. "Maybe not on purpose," he said. "But he did it."

So, basically, my brother was getting his information from a hat, my girlfriend wasn't speaking to me, and my best friend couldn't keep his mouth shut. And it was still the first week of summer vacation, so it was just possible things would get worse.

Cody sat there watching me, the jiggles going up his legs. Then he got this weak smile. "It's seven minus one," he said quietly.

"So?"

Mom quit singing and looked up from her sudoku. "Happy day-before-your-birthday, Cody." Then she glared at me.

"Is there going to be a cake?" Cody asked.

"Of course. I ordered you a special surprise cake from Publix."

My brother hooked his sneaker toes behind the chair rung and leaned toward her. "Shaped like a what?"

She leaned toward him too. "Shaped like a surprise."

"It's not a train, is it?"

"That was your last birthday." She glanced at the hat on the table. "Something you've gotten interested in lately."

Cody looked at it too. "Will it have gray icing?"

Mom stopped with her coffee cup halfway to her mouth. "Did Ben tell you?"

I held up both hands. "Hey, don't look at me! I'm the only one who *can* keep a secret around here."

Cody bounced his heels again. "The hat told me."

Mom picked up her pencil, but stopped. "Are your pants on fire, young man?"

Cody actually looked down to check before he said no.

I snagged a bowl of hummus from the refrigerator and a bag of pitas from the pantry.

I set the bowl down on the table, hard. Mom glanced at the wobbling bowl like she was going to say something, then over at the clock on the stove. "I'd better get ready for work."

"The hat cake was your mom's idea," Dad said quietly as she went up the stairs. "Personally, I liked last year's train a whole lot better."

175

"How come?" Cody asked.

"Let's just say I'm not a big fan of the hat."

"Me either." I fell into a chair and dug a pita into the hummus. "His imagination's been going weird places ever since he found it—weirder than usual, I mean."

Dad rested his arms on the table. "Why are you in such a good mood, Ben?"

I shrugged, then stared at Cody, warning him to keep his mouth shut. "Couldn't sleep. That was some storm we had last night."

"What storm?" Cody spun in his chair and stared out the window. A big shiny puddle sat in the low spot on the driveway.

Dad rolled his shoulders. "Guys? I'm not going to work today. I'm headed over to G-mom and G-dad's, to do an oil change, eat cookies, and swim in their pool. Who wants to ride along?"

"Me!" Cody's hand shot up. "I'll go!"

I shoved another bite of hummus and pita in my mouth.

"How about you, Ben?"

I grunted a no.

"Seriously, what's up with you today?" Dad asked.

Cody leaned toward Dad. "Girlfriend trouble."

I kicked him under the table.

"Girlfriend trouble?"

Why did Dad have to say everything so loud? The last thing I needed was Mom to get into the act.

"Sorry to hear that, Ben. You want to talk?"

"No."

"Sometimes it helps to get a little advice from an old pro."

"An old pro? Dad, you married your one and only girlfriend."

He tipped his chair back and folded his hands over his stomach. "Yup. My record is perfect. No girlfriend trouble ever."

"You should come with us," Cody said to me.

"Yeah," said Dad. "Moping around won't do you any good."

"I'm not moping! I'll read or something."

"Suit yourself." Dad nodded at my brother. "More cookies for us," he whispered. "Plus, we can work on our awesome cannon-balls."

Dad got up from the table and stretched, his rising shirt show-ing off his hairy belly—something to look forward to if I take after him. "Put on your swimsuit, Cody. Meet me back in this kitchen in five and we'll hit the road. I'd appreciate it if the hat stayed here."

"Check," said Detective Dobbs, and he trotted up the stairs.

Dad looked at me like he was about to launch into a lecture. Instead he stood and pushed his chair in. "Feel free to change your mind."

I was still eating hummus when Cody slapped down the stairs in his red swim trunks and flippers. "Do you really need to wear the flippers in the car?" I asked.

"They're not for the car." Cody banged out the door.

When Dad came in wearing his trunks, I pointed out the win-dow. "This is the kind of stuff I put up with every day. I think I deserve a raise."

But Dad just smiled at Cody stomping the water out of the pud-dle. "At least he's not wearing the hat."

෧෨

Just like that, I was brother free, but still stuck in park. I glanced down at my bare chest. I'd put on a shirt and then think of some-thing to do. I took the stairs two at a time, but slowed when I came to Cody's open door. The hat hung on the bedpost, the postcard still jammed under the band.

I walked in, lifted my uncle's hat off the post, and dropped it on my head. It landed covering one eye but I nudged it up, then glanced at myself in the mirror over his dresser. "Not bad." I walked toward myself, checking the hat out. It wasn't sitting quite right, so I pinched the crown, lifted it, and put it on again. I ran the brim between my fingers. "Pretty sharp." It fit me way better than it fit Cody.

Bet Cass would like the way I looked in it. If Cass was speaking to me.

I took the hat off, about to hang it back up, when I saw the package on the dresser—a birthday present for Cody. I was amazed Cody hadn't torn into it. Then I noticed it was from Aunt Sandy. That explained it.

Leaned up against the box was an envelope. I set the hat down on the package and picked up the white envelope. It was muddy, the stamp crooked. No return address, but the postmark, which was smudged and smeared, said "Wichita, KA."

Who did Cody know in Wichita? And who, other than me, would threaten him with monkeys flying out of his butt?

I looked up, considering. There, reflected in the mirror, was the monkey-butt threat and the back of the postcard that stuck up from the hatband. The writing was the same.

I saw my eyes go wide in the mirror. The birthday card was from Uncle Paul, and he was in Wichita.

My hands started to shake. It wasn't addressed to me, and Cody would open it tomorrow. For him it would be no big deal, just one more happy birthday. For me? Maybe it would explain things, things that still bugged me three years after they happened. When Uncle Paul lived with us, he and I were together all the time. Like Cody tags along after me, I tagged along after Uncle Paul. While he was here it was like *I* had an older brother. Then he left—"disappeared," if you listen to Cody.

Looking back, "disappeared" is really what it felt like.

"Hang in there, Shotgun!" on a postcard didn't make up for it. I'd explain all that to Cody when I told him I'd opened it. I thought

178

he'd be okay with it. And if he wasn't, I'd remind him why Cass wasn't speaking to me.

I took a deep breath, opened the flap, and slid the card out.

A sad-eyed puppy stared back at me. "FOR A BIG BOY ON HIS SIXTH BIRTHDAY." That'd get Cody—it kind of got me too. Even though Cody was named after him, Uncle Paul didn't know how old he was.

I opened the card, prepared to be disappointed by seeing just a signature, but inside was a long note.

Yo, Cody Paul,

If I'm not reading this over your shoulder I guess I didn't make it for our birthday. Sorry—eat a piece of cake for me, okay?

Tell my big brother I tried to get there. Tell him if you guys lived anywhere else I'd of made it—sorry I can't explain, but that's just how it is.

When you blow out the candles, keep it simple. Wish for no disasters—believe me, they can ruin your day for a long time.

But maybe we're reading this together. My handwriting is so bad I hope so. Anyway, as of right now, I'm on my way.

Your uncle,
Paul Cody

P.S. Give my best to Shotgun.

When I looked up from the note, my eyes in the mirror looked spooked—like Cody had looked spooked pretty much all the time since finding the hat.

Shotgun. Nobody called me that but Uncle Paul.

The note said he'd be right here if we lived anywhere else. And then there was that comment about disasters ruining your day. Maybe Cody was right about Uncle Paul. Maybe he *had* burned that house down. "By accident," I muttered. But that was the excuse you give when you hit a line drive through somebody's front window. When three people die, who cares if it's an accident?

I thought about accidents, about how they could take you by surprise, but how sometimes you could see them coming. Like G-dad always says about Cody, he's an accident waiting to happen.

Seemed like lately things had been blindsiding me—like the truth about Nowhere leaking back to Cass. I could have prevented that disaster by telling her the truth up front.

Yup, do nothing about an accident waiting to happen, and eventually it does. Suddenly I thought about the Sword of Damocles branch hanging over the roof of Nowhere. If I kept on thinking about it and doing nothing, it would fall on the roof, and why let it happen when I could prevent it?

Taking one last look in the mirror, I straightened the hat. "Come on, Super Hat. Let's go avert a disaster."

Justin

The soundtrack in my head is constant, like the Muzak at the grocery store, only with a better playlist.

One time I asked my older brother if he heard music too. He said no; he heard an announcer's voice saying, "Duane Anthony Riggs has just pitched his third perfect game of the season for the Tampa Bay Rays!"

Right now the tune in my head is pretty sad—a slow drip in a minor key, but it's the right soundtrack for what's going on. Ben is mad at me for telling Cody, mad at Cody for telling Cass, and just mad in general. Plus, I didn't get much sleep last night. Thunder and rain pounding the roof kept waking me up. I dozed off solid just as it was getting light. The clock by my bedside says nine fifteen. Usually I'd be at Ben's by now or he'd be here.

Yup. He's mad.

The old cat sleeping on my chest is purring in his sleep, setting a steady rhythm.

As I rub my hand across the Giz's bony ribs, I imagine *his* soundtrack. "Electric can openers," I whisper. "A symphony of electric can openers."

I press a few chords into Gizmo's furry back, playing him like a piano. Slowly his eyes open, and he gives me that look cats do almost as well as girls, the one that says, *Whatever you're doing, cut it out.* He stands up, sways on his rickety legs, and starts sharpening his claws on the front of the US Army T-shirt I wore to bed.

After a couple of light plucks, he digs in.

"Yow!" I want to throw him across the room, but I guess I deserve it for treating him like a keyboard.

I dress quick and ease past my parents' bedroom. The door is open, the bed a mess, but Mom isn't in it so she probably made it to work.

Downstairs, no one's in the kitchen. I check the view out the front window. Dad's car is gone. He's between sales trips, so I'm guessing he's whacking a golf ball at Jake Gaither Golf Course.

I eat some cold pizza, drink one of Mom's Diet Sprites. What to do? Where to go?

Not Ben's. I could go straight to Nowhere and play some piano, but what if Ben's already there? I step out into the steamy heat. The rain that fell down is going up again. The air's all thick like in a bathroom after a hot shower.

I think, cool air, in-tune piano, Jemmie's. She isn't thrilled with me either, but when is she ever? It's worth a try. And maybe I'll tell her, yeah, I'll get my parents over for a concert, although it probably won't happen. Sometimes just getting the two of them in the same room is a major feat of engineering.

When I get to the Lewises', Cass and Jemmie are in their usual spot on the porch swing, two dripping glasses of sweet iced tea on the railing.

They glance up from the books in their laps. Cass bites her lip. She probably wants to ask about Ben, but all she says is hi.

Jemmie looks kind of startled.

I nod at the open books in their laps. "Required reading?"

Jemmie snaps back to the same old Jemmie. "You think I'd read about some old man and the sea for fun?"

When it comes to required reading I'm the last holdout.

"Go on in." Jemmie nods toward the door. "The piano's right where you left it."

That's my invitation to leave. Instead I stare at her. The music in my head squeals to a stop. Jemmie has these flecks of yellow in her brown eyes. Have I mentioned that?

I notice the flecks because she's staring back—bet I have pizza sauce on my face or something.

"Go on," she says again. "Nana Grace has been asking where you've been."

Inside, Nana Grace is running an old T-shirt over the piano. "Just shinin' it up for you." She gives the wooden lid that covers the keyboard one last swipe, dusts the bench for good measure, then folds the lid back, exposing the keys. "Go on, child. Play me something."

As I sit down, I take a quick look at myself in the mirror over the piano. No pizza sauce on the face. Nothing new in the zit department. I look okay—at least for me.

Nana Grace watches me slide the bench forward. I put my right thumb on home base, middle C, and strike the note. I know she's waiting for me to play, but I always start with that one note.

"Mmmm...mmm," says Nana Grace as the note dies out. "Can't nobody play C the way you do, Justin Riggs."

"Thanks." I can't get my parents to even notice my music. All I have to do is play middle C to get Nana Grace's seal of approval.

As she walks into the kitchen shaking her head over my natural talent, I begin searching out a melody, and I wonder if Jemmie is listening too. Or if maybe my music'll just bother her while she reads.

I don't know how long I've been playing when I feel a hand

brush across the back of my damp T-shirt—and for a second I think it might be Jemmie.

"You got the gift, child," Nana Grace says softly. "You surely do got the gift." The hand gives my arm a light slap. "Bet you also got an appetite." She doesn't wait for an answer, just walks across the room and sticks her head out the front door. "Girls? Come on in for lunch now."

It's lunchtime? My stomach rumbles. Guess so.

"Can you stay?" Jemmie asks as the girls come inside.

Is she giving me a too-bad-I-have-to-invite-you look or an I'd-really-like-you-to-stay-for-lunch look? I consider taking a chance and saying yes, but I'd be eating in front of her—not a fast snack, but a meal at a table, talking with my mouth full, public chewing. "Thanks, but I gotta do something with Ben."

"Oh." Cass wraps her arms around herself. "Would you tell him I said 'hi'?"

"Sure." It isn't much, just two letters, but it might make Ben feel better. "Anything else?"

"Just hi." She tucks her hair behind her ears. "Hi and…I guess I wouldn't mind talking to him sometime."

"Okay, I'll tell him. He wouldn't mind talking to you either," I add fast. I know Ben will be in a crappy mood until he does. "Thanks for the lunch invitation. Bye, Nana Grace. I'll see you guys later."

"Don't forget the 'hi' for Ben," Cass says.

I point at the pocket of my shorts. "Got it." As I turn away I hear a laugh. Sounds like Jemmie's.

Luckily, I'm halfway down the front steps before my stomach lets out another loud growl.

I consider going home. At the moment there's stuff in the fridge, but I have supplies at the hideout, too, and a "hi" and a "wouldn't mind talking" to pass on to Ben if he's there.

It isn't as hard to get to Nowhere as it was when we first found it. We've stomped out a rough path, but everything is still wet after the rain, and I have to sidetrack around a few muddy spots. As I get closer I listen for Ben. He makes noise, especially when he's on a project.

I catch my first glimpse of the roof between the trees, but the woods are still free of Ben commotion. Wondering if he's even there, I begin to whistle the tune in my head.

I stop. Something looks different. I let out a low whistle. The dead branch, the Sword of Damocles that always looms over the roof and bugs Ben, is gone. While I was playing piano, he probably cut it down and then went home for a shower. No reason to go to the hideout if Ben isn't there. I'll catch him at home. The tuna-forked-out-of-a-can lunch I had in mind will be beat by whatever Ben's throwing together at his place.

But as I turn to go, I hear something. It isn't the *cheepy-cheep* of a bird or some other nature sound. It sounds more like a groan.

When I don't hear it again, I shrug and take a step toward home.

"Jus…" My name sounds like another groan.

"That you, Ben?" I turn and jog toward our hangout, but don't see him. He must be around the back.

I almost lose the lunch I didn't eat when I find him. The scraped trail through fallen leaves shows where he dragged himself over to the tree. He's managed to pull himself into a sitting position against the trunk. His shirt is off. One pants leg is soaked in blood. So is the shirt he has pressed against his thigh.

"You okay?" I ask, like an idiot. But there's a lot of blood and I'm not good with blood.

He nods toward the chainsaw that lies a few feet away, the blade partway buried in the ground. Cody's magic hat sits right next to it. "I slipped on the wet roof. The saw got my leg on the way down."

He stares at the wadded-up T-shirt in his hands. I do too. The little wrinkles on his knuckles look like they've been traced with a red pen. "I can't…stop the bleeding."

My stomach flips and I hope I'm not going to be sick as I watch a fat drop of blood splat onto the ground. "Let me." I kneel and put my palms flat against the bloody T-shirt and press down. "Pays to have a plus-size friend, right?"

His blue lips turn up in a half smile. "Funny," he whispers.

"Yup, that's me, Mr. Funny," I babble. "By the way, Cass says hi."

"Really? Tell her I say…hi back."

"First chance I get." I lean hard. Blood is still dribbling down the side of his leg. "What do I do, Ben? Tell me!"

His eyes close.

"No, wake up, Ben! Think health class. Think first-aid films. Come on, Ben," I beg. "Tell me what to do!" He knows I slept through the first-aid videos in health class.

He shakes his head. "Told Dad I needed a cell phone. He wouldn't listen."

"Ben? You're bleeding, big-time."

His head falls back against the tree trunk. "Dad's gonna kill me for taking the chainsaw."

"Come on, Ben! What do we do?"

I'll do whatever he says, but he has to come up with something.

"How about…a nap? I'm tired." His eyelids drift shut.

"No!" For a second I pretend this is a video game. In my head, Ben loses some points, then leaps to his feet. "Ben?" I stare at my bloody hands—Ben is headed for Game Over. "I need instructions, like, right now!"

"Guess I'll never get my driver's license," he mumbles.

I yank my T-shirt over my head and wrap it around Ben's blood-soaked shirt, then tie it as tight as I can behind his leg. "Now what?"

"Go. Get help."

Seems like a good idea for about three seconds, then the first spot of blood comes through my shirt-bandage. "There's no time."

He waves a bloody hand. "Just go. I'll rest while..." His eyelids close again.

"Ben? Ben!" I glance around at trees and more trees and Cody's monument to a bunch of dead people. "Hey! Can anyone hear me?" I yell. "Anybody out there? I need help!"

Someone who knows what to do *has* to show up, like, right now. This can't be up to me.

Hearing a rustle, I whip around. It's just a bird, scratching through the leaf litter looking for lunch. No one is coming.

"Think," I mutter.

What are my options?

Stick with what I'm doing now? I glance down. Now *my* T-shirt is soaked too.

Go for help? But if I quit applying pressure he could die; I don't need a first-aid video to figure that out.

I can't go for help and I can't keep doing what I'm doing. There has to be something else. I swallow hard.

There is.

My brother tried it out on me once when he was on leave from basic training. It's called a "fireman's carry." Firemen don't use it anymore, something about there being too much smoke and heat when you carry a victim up that high, but it's still used in the military to get an injured soldier off the field.

Duane—especially after lots of one-armed push-ups for the sarge—is in great shape. Before I knew what was happening I was hanging across his shoulders. Then, being an instructional kind of brother, he'd showed me the steps.

"Ben." I shake my injured buddy's shoulder. "I gotta get you on your feet."

He slaps at me. "Go away."

"Stand up!" I put my hands under his armpits and try to drag him to his feet. I get him halfway up, then pin him to the tree by shoving my head into his stomach—my hands are still in his armpits, trying to keep him from sliding back down. "Straighten your knees," I pant.

I hear the sound of his back scraping the bark as he pushes up, and—he's doing it! "Steady…steady." Before he can fall over, I drop to my knees and turn sideways to him as he topples. Just like Duane showed me, I have one of his arms draped over my shoulder, a leg draped over the other. The bad leg is hanging down my back, which is good, because me grabbing his bleeding leg would have to hurt. To hold him in place, I grip the leg and arm in the front, hard.

All I have to do now is stand up.

"Sorry about this. It's probably going to hurt." And by that I mean hurt both of us, because now I have to lift his full weight and my own. "One…two…three."

He lets out a moan as I lurch to my feet.

"You're killing me, Jus." He says that sometimes when I make him laugh, but he isn't laughing this time.

"No choice. I have to get you out of here."

"Put me down. Right…now."

"Can't do that." I fall forward a step. "You're heavier than you look."

"Lighter than I was…this morning."

"Hey, funny is my department." Man, I should save my breath. I think I'm going to faint.

I peer ahead, imagining Leroy cutting between the trees, all strong and in shape. Duane's about a million miles away, but Leroy could happen—*if* we'd told him about Nowhere, and *if* he wasn't doing time in summer school.

I'm not strong *or* in shape, and Ben is *way* heavier than he looks.

I stagger forward. "Hey, Ben, this is like a summer camp relay race gone bad." He doesn't make a sound. "Not that I've ever been to camp."

His bare skin feels clammy and cool against my back, and suddenly he's slipping off my shoulders. "Ben, you gotta try to stay up there." I bend forward and yank hard on his arm and leg, but he doesn't make a sound.

Hunchbacked and panting, I travel as fast as I can, my brain jittering. What if I drop him, or trip over a root? What if he dies while I'm carrying him? What if he's dead already?

"Ben, say something."

I'm glad when he groans, overjoyed when he says, "You walk like...Frankenstein."

"I take it that's not a compliment."

He doesn't answer. I feel something warm and wet on my back and realize it's my best friend's blood. Can't think about it.

I stagger toward help, but there are so many trees and brambles and low spots to stumble into, we don't seem to be getting any closer.

"Hey, I forgot. Cass says she'd like to talk." I thought that would get an answer, but it doesn't.

The path that sketches through the trees goes on and on. My lungs are ready to bust out of my chest.

I'm not going to make it.

Story of my life—I try and I fail. I don't try and I fail.

Justin Riggs carrying Ben Floyd more than a few feet? Stupid idea. Doomed. There must've been a better way, but Ben is the idea man. I'm the guy who says, "Sounds good to me," and goes along. Now I'm killing him.

"Ben?" When he doesn't answer I squeeze his arm. "Say something!"

"Okay, okay, I'm up," he mumbles.

Through a break in the trees I see the shiny black of a hot tar road. I can't believe it.

The maroon metal of a battered pickup flashes by. "Hey!" I yell, lurching forward.

Missed that one, but another car'll come along any second.

Has to.

jemmie

The sun beat down as we walked along, watching our feet. Cass hadn't said a word since we left my house and we were almost to the edge of the neighborhood.

"Justin made it sound like Ben *wanted* to talk to me," Cass said finally. Like I figured, she'd been thinking about Ben the whole time.

"Yeah." He might've just said it to make her feel better—Big is like that. A trickle of sweat ran down my spine. "Sure is hot."

Cass didn't answer, just lifted her hair off her neck, probably making up what she was going to say to Ben when we got to Nowhere.

Under my breath, I hummed the tune Big had been playing.

Cass stopped. "You think this is a good idea?"

"Talking to Ben? Sure." I gave her a shove. "You'll be miserable till you do." She went back to walking, eyes on the ground. Bet she was doing the he'll-say-and-then-I'll-say thing in her head.

I squinted, peering across the sunlit street toward the opening of the path we'd beaten down, so I was the one who saw them first. With the glare of the sun, it was hard to figure out what had just crashed out of the trees. I shaded my eyes. "Big?" I breathed. "Big!" I yelled. Then I *ran* across that road—forget looking both ways.

Big's bare chest was heaving as he rolled Ben off his shoulders and into the weeds at the side of the road. "Oh no!" Blood streaked his white skin. "What happened, Big?"

"Chainsaw accident...at the hideout," he gasped.

Cass dropped to her knees next to Ben, who lay real still. She knelt over him and started to cry.

Big's hand was suddenly in my face. "Jemmie, give me your phone!"

I snatched the cell out of my pocket. "Want me to—"

He grabbed it and punched in 911. I watched him, ready to take over—I'm a nurse's daughter. "What is your emergency?" I coached.

He turned away, listening to the operator.

"My friend Ben Floyd had an accident with a chainsaw." Big turned back to me and pointed down. I needed to pay attention to Ben, not him.

Cass had Ben's head in her lap and she was dripping tears on his face—a lot of help that was.

I checked on Ben—I'd never seen so much blood. Neither guy had a shirt on—looked like both shirts were bandaging the wound. I thought I'd have to redo it, but when I knelt down I could see Big had tied it good and tight. It was soaked through. All I could do was put my hands on it and press down. The blood felt sticky and warm as it seeped through my fingers. I stared at Ben's chest, trying to see if it was moving, but I couldn't tell for sure.

Never letting up the pressure on Ben's leg, I talked to God the way Nana Grace does sometimes. *Please, God. Get that ambulance here quick.* Sometimes trains block the road into the neighborhood. *No trains, God. Not now.*

"We're at the corner of Rankin and Rockwell," Justin said to the 911 dispatcher. "We need help right now. He's lost a lot of blood." He listened for a moment, then said, "Ben Floyd. He's thirteen."

Cass, Big, and me pounded up the steps yelling for Nana Grace. She took one look and pressed her hand to her heart. "Sweet Jesus! What on earth?"

Big was too out of breath and Cass was crying, so I told Nana about Ben and how Big had carried him out of the woods.

"The ambulance took Ben." Cass swiped her eyes with her wrist. "They wouldn't let us ride along."

"Y'all would've been in the way. They know what they're doing." She put a hand on Cass's back. "Come on inside and wash up, all of you." She took a hard look at "all of us," like she was counting heads. "Where's Cody?"

"Don't know," Big puffed.

Nana shook her head. "I have to get hold of the Floyds, but one thing at a time." She put ice in glasses—she said we all needed to cool down.

Cass and I washed up first, sharing the kitchen sink. The water off my hands ran pink down the drain.

"Ben'll be okay," Nana said. Then she rested a hand on Big's shoulder, sweat and all. "You sure are brave. Strong too. You saved that boy's life."

Cass wailed. None of us, except Nana Grace, was sure Ben was still alive, but if he was, my grandmother was right. Big had saved him.

While Nana went into the living room and called the Floyds, Big took his turn at the sink. His back to us, he told us what had happened before he and Ben made it to the road. Cass listened with her head down on the kitchen table. I wondered how Big had carried Ben all that way.

The water ran and ran. His arms were shiny-clean but he stayed where he was, facing the sink.

"Jemmie?" Nana said, coming back in the kitchen. "You think you can find that boy a shirt?"

"Yes, ma'am." I had plenty of T-shirts, but none of them were big enough. Instead I went to Mom's room. She still had Dad's T-shirts from his band, "The Mighty." I'd tell her we didn't have anything else to give him, nothing big enough and not girly, but the truth was, I wanted him to wear it. At least today, he *was* mighty.

෨

I'd never been at the Floyds' at night, and I'd never heard the house so quiet. I could've turned on the TV, but it didn't seem right, so I sat at the kitchen table listening to the refrigerator hum. I could hear Cass talking to Cody upstairs. He was too old for tucking in, but after what had happened, he needed it.

As soon as they got the call, the Floyds had rushed to the hospital. Now everyone was there—Ben's parents and grandparents, even my mom. They said Ben would be okay, but he'd lost a lot of blood and would have to spend the night in the hospital.

Cass and me were watching Cody until Mr. Floyd got home. Ben's mom would spend the night in the hospital with Ben.

I stood up and wandered through the house. Ben's basketball was on the coffee table. He wouldn't be needing that for a while. I snuffed and wiped my nose with my wrist. *To Kill a Mockingbird* hung on the arm of the sofa.

It was on my list too. Guess I could hold his place with something and start reading, but I just hung it over the sofa again and kept walking through the rooms.

As I passed the front door for the third time, I jumped. A man stood on the porch, peering in. My heart pounding, I stared right at him. He had a scraggly beard and a skinny face. Nana Grace would probably want to feed him, but to me it looked like a face

194

that should hang on the post-office wall with the word "Wanted" under it. What was he doing looking in the Floyds' window?

He gave me a confused smile and shrugged, then pointed like he was asking if he could come in.

I glanced at the door—it wasn't locked. All he had to do was turn the knob.

I smiled as I walked over. He smiled wider, showing off a broken tooth. When I got to the door I snapped the lock. "Get away from this door!" I yelled. "I'm calling the police!"

"Jemmie, what's going on?" Cass called from upstairs. "Stay here, Cody," she ordered, but I heard two pairs of feet run down the stairs.

The guy on the porch held up both hands and began backing away. "Sorry," he said. "I thought the Floyds lived here. Don't call the cops, please." As he swung around I saw a beat-up pack slung over his shoulders.

Cody, still in his socks, slid across the floor. "Who's out there?"

Cass stared out the window over my shoulder. "Did that guy try to break in?"

"He was looking through the window. But he mentioned the Floyds like he knew them."

"Wait!" Cass pressed a palm to the glass. "That looks like Uncle Paul."

Cody grabbed the knob and tried to jerk the door open. By the time I got it unlocked, the guy had disappeared into the dark.

Cody fell out onto the porch in his pj's.

"Uncle Paul!" he bawled. "Come back, Uncle Paul!"

Even after Cody had yelled him back onto the porch, Uncle Paul still seemed like he was ready to take off.

"Don't worry," I said. "I didn't call the police."

He heaved a sigh and came inside. In the living room, he plopped down on the sofa and rubbed his eyes. "God, am I tired."

I saw Cody bite his lips—he knew no one should take the Lord's name in vain.

Uncle Paul glanced around. "Where are the big people? And where's Shotgun?"

We told him about Ben and the accident in the woods.

"Wait." He sat up straight. "Where did this happen?"

Cody sat down cross-legged on the floor in front of him. "We better tell him the whole story, starting with the hat."

"You tell it," Cass said. "You're the hat-finder."

Cody went all the way back to the basketball game Ben wouldn't let him play. Uncle Paul grinned and said big brothers could be a real pain, but when Cody got to the part about finding the boarded-up building in the woods, he slumped over and put his head in his hands.

Cody tugged the leg of his dirty jeans. "What's wrong, Uncle Paul?"

"Nothing." He dragged a hand down his face. "Go on."

He listened to the rest of the story without looking up.

When we'd told him everything, he flopped back against the sofa, his legs out straight. "The nightmare never ends."

Cody nodded once, like he knew what his uncle was talking about. I sure didn't, but I wasn't about to ask. Like Nana Grace would say, Uncle Paul didn't seem quite right.

But maybe he was just tired and hungry—he was skinny as a stray cat. I fixed him some scrambled eggs, Cass made toast. Cody sat with him, talking.

While we cooked, Cass and me whispered about whether or not we should go home now that there was an adult in the house—but we weren't sure if Uncle Paul counted as an adult, so we decided to stay.

When we came out of the kitchen with the food, Uncle Paul was staring at the ceiling.

"Think he's asleep with his eyes open," Cody whispered. "He's been doing that for a while."

"Not asleep," said Uncle Paul. "Thinking." We put the plates down on the coffee table in front of him and he said thanks. Then he patted his shirt pocket and slid out a pack of cigarettes. He lit one, then glanced around. "Still no ashtrays." He knocked the ash off into his own hand.

No one told him no smoking in the house, not even Mr. Floyd when he came home from the hospital.

At first Mr. Floyd just stood there staring.

But after a few seconds, he opened his arms and bellowed, "Welcome home, Paulie!" Then he suffocated his brother in a big bear hug, knocking ashes onto the rug.

sunday
(seven)

CODY

ody's skin itched with chlorine. No bath the night before. No "Good night, Sport!" from Dad. No knock on the wall between his room and Ben's. No as-usual anything since G-mom came out to the pool saying Ben was in the hospital.

Cody threw off the sheet and sat up in bed. Today was his birthday, but it didn't feel like it, not without a brother around to give him a pinch to grow an inch or a choke so he wouldn't smoke. Dad had said Ben would be okay, but he'd looked worried. And he wouldn't let Cody visit because they didn't want him to see his brother getting stuff pumped into him with tubes.

None of this would've happened if he'd told Mom and Dad about Nowhere.

He didn't think anyone was making breakfast pancakes, but he sniffed to make sure. He smelled cigarettes. That's when he remembered Uncle Paul was here—today was Uncle Paul's birthday too. He was downstairs right now, sleeping on the sofa—or else smoking.

Cody had heard his father and uncle talking for a long time after he was sent up to bed. Their voices had woken him up a couple of times, but now the house was quiet. He glanced at the pineapple bedpost. No hat. Dad didn't like the hat. Maybe he'd told Ben to get rid of it while they were at the pool yesterday.

But probably not. If you were in trouble with Dad, you knew

it, like the time Ben slugged a line drive through Mr. Baker's window. Dad had thrown out the ball, the bat, and Ben's cleats right in front of him.

Last night, even with Ben in the hospital, even with Uncle Paul in the room, he'd parked Cody before sending him up to bed and asked him why he hadn't told about Nowhere.

Cody had answered that Ben said not to tell. And Dad had asked him if he'd jump off a cliff if Ben said to.

"Probably," Cody whispered now, staring at the empty bedpost. "At least if he jumped first."

Cody wished he could put the hat on now. Detective Dobbs was way smarter than he was. But if Dad hadn't told Ben to get rid of the hat, he didn't know what had happened to it. He just knew that it felt gone, like sometime during the day while he'd been belly-flopping and eating cookies it had flapped off the bedpost and flown away.

Sometimes he *had* wished the hat would disappear. He felt bad about that now. He'd thought that when he turned seven, he'd know what to do without it, but seven didn't seem all that different from six. He needed the hat to whisper to him that Ben would be fine… and to tell him what to do next.

He pulled on his yesterday clothes, then stood at the top of the stairs and listened to the tick of the clock on the mantel downstairs.

He could see the sofa and the rumpled pink blanket. It didn't look like anyone was under it, but he couldn't tell for sure. He hopped down the steps on his lucky-left but slid his hand down the banister, resting his weight so he wouldn't make noise.

When he got closer, Cody could see that the only thing on the couch besides the blanket and a pillow was Uncle Paul's dingy green backpack with the frayed straps. He glanced out the window, and the car was in the driveway. Dad was still at home, probably sleeping in after staying so late at the hospital. But where was Uncle Paul?

Cody put a hand on the dirty canvas, and it was almost like he was wearing the hat. Suddenly he knew. Uncle Paul was visiting his nightmare. And Cody knew—just as if the hat had told him—that something bad was about to happen.

He let out a hiccup as he jammed his bare feet into the sneakers he'd kicked off next to Dad's chair. Hiccupped again as he let himself out the door. He didn't even leave a note. He was seven now and, like Dad had said, sometimes you have to decide for yourself. If he did the right thing and left a note, he'd get there too late—and that made leaving a note the wrong thing.

Cody closed the door real quiet, then ran. Way down the block, he realized that he should've asked Dad to come along.

He needed a grown-up—a grown-up would know what to do. Maybe he'd see Nana Grace in front of her house, but he didn't. Mr. Barnett's light was on, but Mr. Barnett didn't like kids.

Cody's shoes felt loose. When he looked down, the laces were flying—but he couldn't waste time tying.

The more he ran, the looser they got, until the sneakers were flopping against his heels.

When he ran out of the left one, he stopped and retied both of them, but he didn't sit on the curb even long enough to catch his breath. He jumped up, pounded across Rankin, and cut into the woods.

Cody hurried along the now-familiar path for the first time by himself. The rising sun flickered between the trees as he stumbled into the clearing where the burned-down house had stood.

When he got there he stopped, out of breath. "Uncle Paul?"

His uncle sat slumped, his back against the front wall of Nowhere—the hat covering his face. "Uncle Paul? Are you okay?"

His uncle shoved the hat brim up and peered at Cody.

"Hey, the hat found you!" Cody blurted.

"Nope, I found it near where your brother fell." His eyes traveled to the spot where Dad's chainsaw stuck out of the ground, then shifted back to Cody. "Just don't go over there."

"Why not?"

"Don't go over there," his uncle repeated. "By the way, happy birthday, Cody Paul."

"Same to you, Uncle Paul Cody."

Uncle Paul stared across the opening in the woods, his eyes on Cody's monument. "Thanks, but I'd rather forget about my birthday."

"Are you kidding?" Cody whooped. "We're going to have a party and cake and…you know…birthday stuff." He trailed off when he realized his uncle was staring at the place where the burned-down house had been.

"Sorry, but 'happy' and 'birthday' just don't go together for me. Haven't for quite some time."

Cody wanted to ask, *Did you burn that house down?* but he couldn't ask an uncle he just met a question like that. He had to say something, though. "Hey, you know what? Your socks don't match."

As Uncle Paul folded his legs for a look, his knees poked out of the tears in his jeans. "They sure don't. But I bet I have another pair just like this one in my pack."

Cody trotted over and sat down opposite his uncle. "So, what should we do on our birthday?"

Uncle Paul shrugged, then lit a cigarette. But instead of letting the flame on the lighter go out, he watched it dance. "We could burn this old building down."

Cody blinked hard. "For really?"

His uncle let the flame go out, but the lighter stayed in his hand. "I can't shake this place, Cody Paul. I might feel better if it was gone." His head fell back against the wall, and he stared straight ahead at the house that wasn't there. "It's not like anyone is in it. It's just an old building stuffed with junk."

"But you want to *burn* it down? After what happened…you know…the last time?"

"It'd do the job. This place is bad, real bad. Can't you feel it?"

Cody put a hand on the wall, patting it like a dog. "It's a good old building."

His uncle snorted. "This 'good old building' has haunted me for years. I was sure it had fallen in by now." He slapped the wall hard. "But nope, it's still solid, still doing its stuff." He opened his eyes so wide, Cody could see little red veins. "Yesterday it almost killed my buddy Shotgun."

Cody thought about it. "The building didn't make Ben take Dad's chainsaw and use it up on a slippery wet roof, Ben did."

"I can tell which Floyd brother *you* take after." He sucked on the cigarette like it was the only way to get air. "Hope you're not about to give me the 'personal responsibility' lecture." Uncle Paul's hand shook as he held the cigarette an inch away from his lips.

"Nope."

"Good." He took another deep drag. "I already got it last night."

"From Dad?"

"Yup."

"He gave it to me last night too."

"Yeah, I heard it."

Cody nodded. "He does it the best."

Uncle Paul's laugh exploded like a sneeze, then he rubbed his lips with the back of his wrist. "Sorry. It makes me kind of crazy being here." He blew out a big cloud of smoke, twisting his lips so the smoke came out sideways, not right in Cody's face.

Breathing shallow, Cody leaned toward him. "Uncle Paul, are you okay?"

"Sure, sure." Uncle Paul stared at Cody's monument. "Make

that a no. If falling off the roof was Ben's fault, then that"—he jabbed the cigarette toward the charred slab—"was mine."

"How come?" Cody leaned toward his uncle, about to get the story the hat had only whispered about.

"My buddy Cole and I were sleeping in this good old building the night of the fire. It was my birthday."

"Like today."

"Yeah, just like today. Cole gave me a mess of fireworks. I set them off. I wouldn't even let him light one since they were my birthday present, so I can't say to myself, maybe he did it." He dragged a hand down his face. "One of the spinners must've landed on the roof. I guess it took a while to catch on. When we woke up, the light through the window was so bright, I thought it was morning. Then I smelled the smoke."

Cody leaned toward him. "It was an accident. You didn't mean to set the house on fire."

"Tell that to Lucy."

"Maybe we can."

Uncle Paul jumped. "Like how?"

Cody reached over and touched the brim of the hat with one finger. "I'll need this."

"The hat? Why?"

"It tells me things," Cody said.

Uncle Paul took off the hat and held it in both hands. "It's just a hat, Cody. I bought this for an interview for a job I didn't even want. I thought they'd take one look at the hat and write me off as a goof, but they gave me the job."

"Dad got you the interview."

"He did." Uncle Paul ran the brim between his fingers. "Your dad may not believe this, but once I got the job I tried to make it work. I knew what it meant to him, but I just couldn't." He plopped the hat on Cody's head. "Here. It's all yours now. Happy birthday."

"Thanks." Cody pushed the hat back. "But it's…well…a big responsibility."

Uncle Paul leaned back on his arms. "Felt that way to me when I wore it too."

"Really? Did it…tell you stuff?"

"Yeah, it told me I was going to work in an office without windows for the next forty years."

"Not stuff like that."

"That's what it said to me. What does it tell you?"

"Secret stuff. Didn't it ever do that to you?"

"Can't say that it did. I just remember it made me feel like a kid wearing my dad's hat."

"Me too." Cody's head began to sweat under the hat. "Or my uncle's."

Uncle Paul leaned in so close Cody could smell stale cigarettes on his breath. "So what's the hat got to say for itself now?"

"Just a sec." Cody tapped the hat, dropping it over his face. He closed his eyes and waited for some hat wisdom, but no words came to him. The hat hardly ever flooded his head when he needed it to.

With no word from the hat, he started to worry. Back at the house, Dad was probably waking up. Maybe even walking into his room singing "Happy Birthday to You!" Dad would be scared when he found his son's bed empty.

"Anything?" Uncle Paul asked.

Cody crinkled his face, concentrating, stalling. "I'm beginning to…you know…get something." When he looked down he could see his uncle's hands, the cigarette shaking in his fingers, his fingernails chewed worse than his own.

"Well?"

Cody *was* getting something, but it wasn't coming from the hat. It was coming from his uncle.

Uncle Paul was sadder than any of the dead people's stuff in the monument. That sadness seemed washed out like a road-chalk drawing after it rained. Uncle Paul's sadness was right now. The lighter clicked and the flame danced.

"The hat says they forgive you," Cody blurted out. "Especially Lucy."

Justin

It's here at last, Cody's big day. Seven! The countdown is over. But the countdown isn't the only thing that's over. Having a place of our own is over. Me having a piano—over. Ben being ungrounded—history.

Jemmie called me last night after babysitting the little dude while the Floyds were at the hospital. She's never called me before, but does it count if all she had to say was that Ben would be okay and that the mysterious Uncle Paul had mysteriously reappeared?

I'm relieved about Ben, and sort of neutral about the uncle, but I know the call from Jemmie was nothing personal. With Ben out of commission and Nowhere off-limits, it's like summer's already over, even though it's hardly begun.

I'm walking aimlessly around the neighborhood when I find myself on Jemmie's block. The girls are sitting on Jemmie's porch swing. I say, "Hey." They hey me back, but they sound like I feel.

Jemmie invites me up and we sit awhile, the three of us crammed together on the porch swing. She glances at me a couple of times. I know because we glance simultaneously. Finally she says, "You were really brave yesterday."

"More like scared," I admit.

We swing some more, acting like the three of us jammed together isn't awkward.

I suggest we go say our goodbyes to Nowhere while we still have the chance, mostly to get us off the swing. But when we reach our old hideout, Cody and a guy I figure must be the missing uncle are already there, sitting with their backs against the outside wall. The man needs a shave and a trip through the heavy-duty washer at the Laundromat.

Cody handles the introduction. "Jus, this is Uncle Paul."

I nod because I don't know what to call him. "Uh…happy birthday."

Cody thanks me. The uncle says, "Happy unbirthday to you, Jus."

The girls and I go inside. In a second, Cody and the hat follow.

I stare at the piano, thinking how much I'm going to miss it, even if it is out of tune and has lots of silent keys. I turn away, blinking, just as a face appears in the half-open door. "Looks different." The uncle is still outside, but he leans into the room, just a little. "New shelves?"

"Ben did it." Cody slaps one of the shelves his brother put up. "He's like Dad. He builds things."

His uncle leans in further. "Curtains? What's with curtains in the Cave of the Secret Brotherhood?"

Cass twists the front of her shirt. "Sorry. I sewed them."

"On that old machine?" Now the uncle steps inside—and he takes a sharp breath. "Oh, no…no…" Suddenly all shaky, he walks over to the chair Cass always sits in to sew. He lifts the dress that hangs over the back. Holding it at arm's length, he bites his lower lip. Suddenly, he crushes the fabric against his face like he's trying to suffocate himself.

"What're you doing?" Cody's voice is all funny and high.

Uncle Paul's arms drop. Hanging from one hand, the dress drags on the floor. "There was this perfume she always wore… Stupid of me to think I could still smell it after all these years."

Cass hugs herself and twines one skinny leg around the other. "You mean Lucy?"

He nods and swallows hard. "She was sewing this to wear to a dance with me."

"It was a long time ago." Jemmie takes the dress out of his fist and hangs it on the back of the chair again. She runs a finger along a seam. "See how Cass sewed the sleeves on?"

He stares at his empty hand for a few seconds, then pivots and crosses the room, like it takes a massive effort just to lift his feet.

Cody cuts in front of him. "No, don't!"

Uncle Paul is headed for the dresser where Jemmie and I found the fireworks.

He grabs his nephew gently by the shoulders. "Step aside, Cody Paul. It is what it is." When Cody doesn't move, his uncle walks around him.

For a second, Uncle Paul rests his palms on the top of the old chest of drawers, his eyes closed. "You can do this," he says softly. White knees poke through the tears in his jeans as he squats. He grabs the handles and pulls, but the drawer doesn't budge. I could lend him my weight, but I don't want him to open that drawer.

"It's kinda hard," Cody says. "Why don't you just—?" But his uncle gives the drawer a savage jerk. It grinds open with a loud squeal, and the bag of fireworks is there, right on top.

"No..." Uncle Paul's forehead thunks the edge of the chest of drawers like he can't even hold his head up.

Cody rushes over to him. "Uncle Paul? You okay?"

His uncle's shoulders shake.

Cody puts a hand on his back. "You didn't *mean* to do it. It was an accident."

Uncle Paul shudders. Cody pats.

The girls and I trade looks, unsure what to do.

"It's okay," says Cody. "It's now, not then." He reaches around and grabs the bag of fireworks out of the drawer. "We're getting rid of these."

Uncle Paul wipes his eyes on the shoulder of his shirt. "How?"

I can tell that Cody hasn't thought about that. "We can't burn 'em, that's for sure." He looks around. The red shovel that always leans against the wall by the door stands in a beam of light, which in Cody's world is the same as getting a message from some higher power. "I know! We'll bury 'em."

Uncle Paul pushes himself to his feet, then hitches his pants. "Yeah, okay." He wraps his fist around the shovel handle. "But if we're gonna give the past a proper burial, the hole has to be big."

Cody glances down at the bag of fireworks in his hand. I can almost see the question marks floating above his head. The bag is dinky—why dig a big hole?

But I get it. There is more than a bag of spinners that needs burying. "I'll help you," I say.

"Me too!" says Cody. "I've been digging in the backyard finding dinosaurs. We'll take turns."

Soon as we step outside, Cody stomps a spot near the door. "How about right here?"

But Uncle Paul walks over to the foundation of the burned-down house. He stands for a long minute, staring at the monument. "Here." He grinds the shovel blade into the dirt in front of the slab with a hard kick, then throws the dirt over his shoulder.

It's like the guy has a fever, like he can't dig fast enough. He jams the shovel into the ground over and over. Dirt flies, but in no time he's breathing hard.

Cody insists on taking a turn. He tries to throw dirt like his uncle did, and he sprays it out good, but lots of it falls right back in the hole.

After a minute he complains that the shovel is hurting his foot.

Then he lifts an arm to his nose and takes a whiff. "Hey! I can smell my own chlorine!"

Which is better than I'll smell after I take my turn, but I reach for the shovel. Like carrying Ben out of here, this is a job that has to get done. I can tell, looking at Ben and Cody's scrawny uncle, he can't do it alone.

I'm dripping sweat when Uncle Paul reaches for the shovel. I hand it off and climb out of the hole. "How deep are we going?" I ask.

Uncle Paul stares up into the trees, considering. "Center of the earth."

Good thing the soil on this side of town is mostly sand. It digs easy.

"Keep an eye out for dinosaurs," Cody says, sitting cross-legged at the edge of the hole.

Jemmie digs next. Then Cass.

I'm digging when Uncle Paul steps up onto the slab and stands next to the monument. Without touching a thing he circles it slowly, then collapses into a squat, his head resting on his knees.

Even Cody pretends he doesn't notice Uncle Paul is crying, and I keep on tossing dirt out of the chest-deep hole—in the last two days I've done more physical activity than in my entire previous thirteen years.

I'm pretty sure I'm about to die when Jemmie jumps down into the hole and reaches for the shovel. But instead of taking a turn, she holds the shovel still, both hands clenched on the handle. "We've reached the center of the earth—or close enough."

I crawl out of the hole. Jemmie hands up the shovel and boosts herself out too. Cody swings his dangling legs over the edge. "Uncle Paul? It's done."

Finally, Uncle Paul lifts his head. "Deep as a grave," he says. "And that's deep enough." He stands and jumps down into the hole.

Cody passes him the dinky bag of fireworks.

His uncle takes it and sets it down at the bottom of the hole. Even before he points at the monument, I know what's coming. "Everything," he says. "We'll bury it all."

"Not *everything*. Not Sparky's dish!" Cody whines.

"Everything," his uncle repeats.

Piece by piece, we hand Cody's monument down to Uncle Paul.

"Goodbye, scary doll." Cody passes his uncle a burned plastic doll head. The dog dish comes next. "Goodbye, Sparky."

Uncle Paul arranges everything carefully, then climbs out.

The last things from the monument to go into the hole are the two wrought-iron pieces.

Cody and his uncle lower one. Jemmie and I lower the other.

Lying on top of everything, they look almost like a gate. "Guess we put the dirt back now," Cody says.

"Gotta get one more thing," says Uncle Paul, going back inside.

I hear Cass take a deep breath when Uncle Paul comes out with Lucy's dress draped over his arms. He shakes it out, the way Ben's mother flings out a tablecloth she's trying to spread. The wind catches it and the dress dances.

Tears drip off Uncle Paul's chin. Cody holds up an edge of the dress so his uncle can wipe the tears away, but Cass shakes her head and Cody lets go.

Bare knees on the ground, Uncle Paul lays the dress over the curlicues of wrought iron, hiding all the things the fire destroyed. He straightens the sleeves. Then he crosses his arms. "That's all my bogeymen," he says. "Every last one." He squints up at Cody. "Time to get rid of yours." Uncle Paul points, then clicks his fingers. "The hat."

Cody slaps both hands over the hat. "No, it's magic! You can't bury it. And remember? You gave it to me!"

"I did, but it's no good for you, Cody. It takes you funny places and tells you weird stuff. It's time to think for yourself." He peered into the hole. "If I can put all this to rest, you can do it too. It's time to let the magic hat go."

Cody takes the hat off and holds it in both hands. "But it's my hat...." His eyes are shiny.

"How about if you give it to Lucy?" Uncle Paul leans into the hole and puts a hand on the shiny satin. "The hat can keep her company."

This is all getting a little weird, like the dress and the hat are alive.

Hugging the hat, Cody stares into the hole.

"Let her have it," says Cass. "The dress does look lonely."

Cody heaves a sigh and sets the hat down right where Lucy's heart would be if she were wearing the dress. "Goodbye, Lucy, goodbye, hat. Goodbye." He looks around at the rest of us, like he expects something.

So, one after another, we say goodbye to Lucy, goodbye to the hat.

Everyone is too tired to stand, let alone use the shovel, so we push the dirt in with our hands, covering the dress and the hat and everything else. Cody stamps it down.

"Guess that's it," says Uncle Paul.

"No it's not!" Jemmie snatches Uncle Paul's hand, then grabs one of mine. "We have to say a prayer."

We all take hands, forming a small circle.

Holding Jemmie's cool hand in my sweaty one, I'm distracted, but I try to concentrate on the list of things she says God has to do for Uncle Paul and Lucy and even the dead dog—stuff like take care of them and hold them in His light. I hope God doesn't mind being bossed around.

I see Uncle Paul let out a long, slow breath. When Jemmie reaches the "Amen," he repeats it as loud as anyone. Prayer over, we let go and Uncle Paul drapes an arm around Cody's shoulders.

"Come on, Cody Paul. Let's go get us some cake and ice cream."

ben

I left the hospital with Mom about eleven, my leg bandaged, a fold-up walker in the trunk. I sat in the car while she ran into Publix to get my medicine and the big white box with Cody's cake inside.

I knew Uncle Paul was at the house—Dad had called Mom at the hospital. I smiled thinking about it as I sat in the car on the way home—he'd made it back after all.

I felt like an old guy limping up the driveway with the walker. I was watching the ground to be sure I didn't set a walker leg down in a hole when a voice from the porch shouted, "Hey, Shotgun!" I looked up.

He must've been fresh out of the shower. His long hair was wet, plastered to his skinny neck. When he smiled, I saw that one of his front teeth was half-gone. Instead of the cool uncle who took off three years ago, he was like one of the guys who hang out on Tennessee Street waiting for The Shelter to open.

꩜

He sat with me the rest of the day. Between blowing up balloons for Mom, who was going crazy with the birthday-decorating thing, and watching Cody buzz around standing on chairs and taping streamers to the walls, Uncle Paul and I got in a lot of talking. Sitting in Mom's rolling desk chair, I was fairly mobile, so he and I moved to wherever they weren't while he told me his story.

I knew he'd been in Seattle because of the postcard, but after Seattle—which he said was too rainy—he'd gone down the West Coast washing dishes, picking fruit. He was in Mexico for a while. "Best way to learn a new language," he said. He'd camped out in the Sierra Madres for a couple of months, until it got too cold.

In the last three years Uncle Paul had been everywhere—and nowhere—and now he was back.

Kind of embarrassed, he told me about burying everything near the burned-out house. "Took care of a lot of old business," he said. "Maybe now I can get some rest."

"Wish I'd been there to throw in Dad's chainsaw."

He nodded once. "I hear ya."

I took a deep breath and talked soft, even though the birthday tornado raging in the kitchen was loud. "You don't have to tell me if you don't want to, but did you start that fire?"

He patted the pocket with cigarettes in it, then looked around like he'd just remembered where he was. Instead of lighting up, he scrubbed his hands back and forth on the knees of his jeans. "Yeah, I started it."

Then he told me about the fire. The hat hadn't lied—it *was* his fault and it *was* an accident.

"I guess things'll get better now," he said. But even though he'd "buried the past," he still looked twitchy.

"What happened to Cole?" I asked.

"Wouldn't know. I never saw him again after he went to live with his grandparents in Arkansas."

"Do you want to find out?"

He shook his head. "Might be best to let that sleeping dog lie." Then he swallowed so hard his Adam's apple bobbed. "I never saw him after the night of the fire. Bet he blames me for what happened. And what if he's dead too?"

"What if he isn't? You don't need to talk to him or anything, but don't you want to know?" I rolled the desk chair over to Mom's computer and turned it on. I thought he'd tell me not to search for Cole, but when he didn't, I typed "Coleman Branson" into Google. I figured the name was unusual enough that we'd get just one or two hits, but we got half a dozen.

"Holy crap," he muttered when he saw that the first one had a death date on it that was two years old.

"Can't be that guy," I said. "He was born in 1942."

"Gotta be this one," he said, pointing to "Coleman Branson, formerly of Tallahassee."

I clicked and…we'd found him.

Uncle Paul leaned so close to the screen it lit his face with an eerie bluish light. "I don't believe it." Then he laughed and fell back in his chair. "Cole's a podiatrist, a foot doctor! And I thought *I* messed up!"

Even if he spent his time checking out stinky feet, Cole *was* a doctor, but I didn't point out that. It cracked my uncle up so bad he went limp in his chair. I don't think he'd laughed like that in a long, long time.

෨෧

That night, Cody was a basket case. "Is it time to open presents yet?" he asked every five minutes.

"Wait for the others to get here," said Mom.

G-mom, G-dad, and Uncle Paul sat at the dining room table where we'd do the usual singing and Cody would spit the candle flames out.

I sat on Mom's rolling chair, my foot propped up on a stool—

Mom insisted I keep it elevated. Cody was about to lose it when the doorbell did its usual *thunk-clunk*.

"I got it!" Cody dashed out of the room.

"Hey, birthday boy!" Cass's voice. Bet she was giving my "little bother" a hug.

Jemmie and Jus came in and wished him a happy birthday too.

Come on, Cass.... I really wanted to see her, but the birthday boy was slowing her down. I stared toward the other room and waited. The last time I'd seen her I was lying in the weeds at the side of the road with my head in her lap. I knew she was crying because I felt tears falling on my face. At least I thought I did. The next time I opened my eyes, the road was rushing away real fast outside the little rectangular window in the back door of the ambulance.

Cass came in ahead of the other two. She stood for a second in the doorway, then ran over and hugged me. She stepped back quick, though. Hugging in front of everyone was weird. But things were okay between us again, so I guess something good came out of slashing my leg and losing half my blood.

The bad side was, my leg hurt. A lot. Plus, I was under permanent house arrest and Nowhere was off-limits for the rest of my life.

In a few minutes the other three came in too, Cody prancing ahead, his arms full of presents. I picked out Jus's gift right away. It was the one wrapped in an Ace Hardware bag stapled shut.

Good thing Leroy wasn't there. Jemmie and Justin were standing real close together, looking stupid. I bet watching Jus muscle me out of the woods on his shoulders showed her another side of him even I, his best friend, never suspected. Justin the superhero. Now they kept trading stupid looks—another benefit of me almost cutting off my leg.

I was as surprised as Jemmie that he'd done it—especially since I'd told him not to. Justin not listening to me was a first. And it saved my life.

Mom passed out pointy birthday hats with elastic bands we were supposed to put under our chins.

"You're kidding, right?" said Uncle Paul, staring at the stupid hat.

"Just put it on, Paulie." Dad knuckled his brother's shoulder. "Sometimes it's easier to go along."

"If you say so." He snapped the hat on.

"Darn it," said Mom. "I don't think I have any matches."

"Helps to know a smoker," said Uncle Paul, tossing her his lighter.

We were all in the dining room with the lights out, waiting for Mom to carry the flaming hat cake in from the kitchen when we heard her say, "I can't believe it!"

"Can't believe what?" Cody yelled. He was sitting on a cushy hassock rolled in from the den, his pointy hat way back on his head.

"I can't believe I didn't look at the cake when I picked it up!"

"Did you accidentally order whole wheat with spinach icing?" I asked.

Cody gave me a worried glance.

"I was kidding," I told him.

"Oh well. I guess it'll have to do." Mom was still in the kitchen when she launched the song. "Happy birthday to you…"

We all sang, Cody the loudest: "Happy birthday to ME, happy birthday to ME!" The candle flames wavered as Mom carried the cake out on a tray.

When she set it on the coffee table, Dad guffawed. "Looks like they misread the writing on the order!"

Sure did. The icing was gray—but that was all they got right.

"I guess it's my fault," said Mom. "My *H* must have looked like a *C*."

"It's okay." Cody leaned over the cake, the candles lighting up his chin. "I like cats."

Before I could tell him to wish for no disasters, he blew out all the candles in one spitty puff.

Mom rested her hands on her thighs, leaned down, and kissed him on the forehead. "Good wish?"

"Supergood wish with cherries on top."

At seven, Cody was as goofy as ever; the pointy paper hat suited him better than the fedora.

I glanced at Dad and his own "little bother," sitting side by side. Maybe warding off disasters is the responsibility of the older brother. Looking at Uncle Paul, I figured out that the job could go on for quite a while—maybe forever. Dad hadn't been there for the really big disaster, but I knew he'd keep on trying.

If Uncle Paul stuck around, Dad would do his best to keep him disaster free. I had another shot with Cody too. Unless I'd lost my summer job.

I hoped I hadn't.

early august

Cass

With Ben out of commission, the Floyds enrolled Cody in the first session of Nature Day Camp down the street at the Tallahassee Museum. By the second session Ben, Justin, Jemmie, and me were down there too, as volunteer junior counselors. According to Ben, he now had a dozen "little bothers" to keep track of. We all complained about the mosquitoes, but mostly we shined ourselves up with spray-on repellent and had a great time.

In the evenings when it was cooler we were back on the street, shooting hoops.

"Shotgun! Over here!" Uncle Paul would wave his arms. "I'm open!" And Ben would pass the ball to him—unless Jemmie intercepted it. Some things never changed.

But plenty had.

We didn't play Girls vs. Guys anymore since Uncle Paul had been added. And Cody. Some nights Ben's dad would play too.

Uncle Paul wasn't big on following the rules. He liked making up his own. It got even more confusing when he brought a second basketball home with him from his part-time job at Sports Authority (my sister said he got the job because of the great haircut she gave him). Next paycheck he came home with a third ball.

Sometimes we had all three balls in play, stealing and shooting nonstop. Uncle Paul wasn't a good player, but he would try anything. He invented new games and made up rules on the spot, like the double-man rule that let Cody sit on someone's shoulders when he was trying for a free throw. Doing that, Cody made his shots most of the time. He said it was better than a magic hat, which was lucky because the magic hat was gone.

And so was Nowhere—I mean, the building was there, but we weren't. That secret place of our own was beginning to feel like something out of a story I'd heard a long time ago. *Once upon a time, in a deep, dark woods...*

Summer was almost gone too and all of us were thinking about what would come next. But that was okay.

Maybe it was time for a change.

ADRIAN FOGELIN is the author of nine titles for middle grade and young adult readers. Open one of her books, and you'll meet the kids in her home neighborhood in Tallahassee, Florida, where she and a band of trusty volunteers maintain the Front Porch Library—where local patrons usually arrive by bike or on foot. Adrian is also a songwriter and half of the musical duo "Hot Tamale."

www.adrianfogelin.com

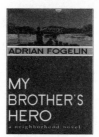

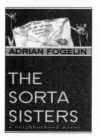